YOUNG HOUDINI

The Silent Assassin

WHO is the silent assassin?

WHY is he targeting members of a charitable society?

WHEN will he strike next?

HOW will Harry escape this time?

Read on to find out!

Note from author, Simon Nicholson

Harry Houdini (1874-1926) was the most famous magician and escape artist of his age—a genuine legend in his own lifetime. He broke free from nailed-shut crates thrown into icy rivers; he escaped from the most secure prisons in America; no straitjacket, padlock, or pair of handcuffs could hold him. His tricks dazzled the world, and mystery surrounded him. How had he acquired such incredible powers? Some speculated that he had made a deal with the supernatural. Others whispered that he was an international spy, or that he dabbled in the affairs of kings and queens. The great Houdini himself was happy to encourage such rumours and wild tales—all part of creating his extraordinary reputation.

But what about Houdini as a boy? A few facts are known—he emigrated from Budapest, Hungary, to America with his family when he was four, and grew up peacefully in Appleton, Wisconsin. No records of anything particularly spectacular. But given all the intrigue that surrounded Harry in his adult life, I began to wonder if perhaps there might have been something mysterious about his boyhood too.

What if those peaceful years in Wisconsin turned out to have been a cover-up, invented later to conceal a far more dangerous and exciting truth? What if Houdini actually moved to America when he was a slightly older boy—and under mysterious circumstances? What if he became separated from his family, and fell in with two friends, not to mention a secretive crime-solving organization? The real Houdini was happy to encourage rumour about himself, remember—not only that, but he did a fair bit of his own tale-spinning too. At one point, he claimed to have been born on American soil, not in Hungary at all; he busily created enigma around the secrets to his tricks; he even hired the famous writer H. P. Lovecraft to write a made-up tale about him having an adventure in Egypt, in which he investigated sinister forces beneath the pyramids...

A hero; a living legend; a man of mystery. And perhaps, I thought, it was time for even more mystery to be revealed—the business of what might have happened to Harry Houdini, daredevil magician, when he was a BOY.

To Harriet and Louis Engelke

OXFORD
UNIVERSITY PRESS

Great Clarendon Street, Oxford OX2 6DP
Oxford University Press is a department of the University of Oxford.
It furthers the University's objective of excellence in research, scholarship,
and education by publishing worldwide. Oxford is a registered trade mark of
Oxford University Press in the UK and in certain other countries

First published 2016

British Library Cataloguing in Publication Data
Data available

ISBN: 978-0-19-274489-0

1 3 5 7 9 10 8 6 4 2
Printed in Great Britain

Paper used in the production of this book is a natural,
recyclable product made from wood grown in sustainable forests.
The manufacturing process conforms to the environmental
regulations of the country of origin.

SIMON NICHOLSON

YOUNG HOUDINI

The Silent Assassin

OXFORD
UNIVERSITY PRESS

Chapter One

Harry gripped the ship's rail. He felt it shudder with the vibrations of the engine, thundering deep in the vessel's insides. Wind whipped through his hair and he looked down at the sea nearly a hundred feet beneath him, churning as the propellers spun below.

'Are you ready, Harry?'

'Perkin's agreed to risk his pocket watch. Are you set?'

Harry lifted his hands. The rail shuddered on, but his fingers, a few inches above it, were steady. He turned towards the boy and girl who had spoken to him, the boy in a neat tweed suit, the girl wearing her usual scruffy smock. Arthur and Billie were running about with buckets, collecting coins from the crowd of passengers who had gathered on the deck. Nearby stood Perkin, a lanky sailor whose face was prickling with perspiration, even though the October wind was hard and cold. In a trembling hand the sailor was clutching a pocket watch on a chain.

'Took ages to persuade him—way tougher than the hat,' said Billie, hurrying past Harry with her bucket.

'You told him I've been practising, yeah?' said Harry.

'Told him? He insisted on knowing. I had to make up a training schedule and everything.' Arthur hurried by, too. 'He's asking for an even bigger cut of the takings, I'm afraid. I said we'd give him half.'

'I suppose it is a pretty valuable pocket watch,' said Harry, crouching down and loosening his bootlaces. As his fingers worked, those familiar sensations arrived, tiny flickers and twitches jumping all over his skin. *Good*, he thought—every flicker, every twitch would help him focus on the trick ahead. Deep in his chest, his heartbeat quickened.

'Ladies and gentlemen, prepare yourselves for the greatest juggling trick of our voyage so far!' Billie had swung round and was addressing the crowd. 'We astounded you as the SS *Morley* chugged out of New Orleans! We dazzled you as she sailed across the freezing Atlantic!'

'And now, as our journey closes, as England draws near—' Arthur joined in, 'the boy called Harry Houdini will astound you with his powers once again.

Come see a juggling trick in which he juggles with his own life! Not much to ask you to pay for, surely? In dollars and cents or British shillings—we accept either currency, you'll be pleased to hear.'

Coins clattered into the buckets, and Harry watched them catch the sunlight as they jumped out of the passengers' hands. *Nice speech, Artie,* Harry thought—and his friend had done a good job with making up that name for him too, thanks to some quick research back in the New York library. Harry switched his attention to the pocket watch, which was shaking as it dangled from Perkin's grip. He walked across to him and held out his hand, but saw the sailor's fist tighten around the watch's chain.

'What if you mess this up?' More sweat gathered on Perkin's face. 'It was my grandfather's, this watch—I reckon it's worth a bunch.'

'Your hat didn't end up in the sea when we did it last time.' Harry pointed up at the hat on Perkin's head, and then down at his feet. 'Your shoes didn't either, the time before that.'

'Hat, shoes—they belong to the shipping line, plenty of spares I could take from the store.' Perkin swallowed, but his fist was loosening; Harry could see that from tiny movements in the muscles of the sailor's wrist. 'The watch is actually mine. I could sell it for proper cash.'

'You'll get plenty of cash from those buckets.' Harry nodded towards his friends. 'Why don't we say you take even more of it—three quarters?'

'Really?' Perkin looked at the buckets, and his fist loosened a little bit more. 'Well, that's mighty fine. Although what about the last bit of the trick, the dancing bit, I don't want . . . WAIT!'

It was too late. His fist had loosened so much that a few of the chain's links had slipped through his hand and Harry had taken that as a signal, his own hand flashing forward, grabbing the watch, and tossing it high in the air. His other hand danced in his pocket, pulling out a leather ball and a teaspoon from the ship's canteen, and Harry began juggling them all in a flying circle. The warm leather brushed against his fingers, followed by the edge of the spoon and then the cool roundness of the watch's metal, as he walked backwards towards the ship's rail.

'See the speed!' Billie addressed the crowd again, still gathering coins. 'See the sureness of his grasp!'

'The slightest slip, and Able Seaman Perkin's watch goes flying!' Arthur joined in. 'And yet Harry edges ever closer to the rail—in fact he's jolly well sitting on it, look!'

Harry had hopped onto the rail and was perched there, still juggling. His unlaced boots hung loosely from his feet, and he flexed his ankles in preparation. He saw the faces of the crowd staring at him, Perkin staring hardest of all, his eyes following the watch. But every now and then, the sailor's eyes darted to the side, towards Arthur's and Billie's buckets, which were steadily filling with coins.

'Pay what you can!' Billie shouted over the gasps. 'Harry will stop at nothing to excite you, remember—even if it means risking his own life!'

'One mistake, and he'll tip off the rail.' Arthur waggled an arm in Harry's direction. 'A hundred feet fall, down to the sea below!'

'And let's not forget the propellers now,' Billie added, nudging a lady with a parasol, who was taking a little too long delving in her purse. 'Each one has five terrible blades, and each blade is the height of a small house.' She nudged the lady again. 'And they spin so fast they are a blur! Nothing can survive their ferocious power, not even—'

'MY WATCH!' yelled Perkin.

Harry had jumped up, and was balanced barefoot on the rail, juggling on. As he jumped, he had kicked off his unlaced boots, and they spun through the air, Billie grabbing one, Arthur the other. *They're not bad catches either*, thought Harry with a smile. His bare toes curled around the rail; those flickers travelled all over his body, and his heart throbbed harder as he heard the crowd scream.

'Someone stop him!'

'He's gone too far!'

'He's just a boy—he'll kill himself!'

'Grab him, someone!'

'Grab him? But that might accidentally push him backwards!'

A bearded old man sank onto the deck with shock. Three bonneted ladies clutched bottles of smelling salts to their noses. In the middle of it all, Harry saw Perkin, his eyes rolling round after the watch, almost as if they were being juggled too. *Now for the interesting bit.* Still juggling, Harry started to dance, a crab-like caper along the slender rail. His bare feet lifted up and down, and swapped places, and scampered on, and each time they landed he felt the trembling of the rail caused by the vibrations of that vast engine, powering those enormous propellers, waiting for him in the sea below. *Nearly done.* He danced back along the rail. *No need for Perkin to have worried about the dancing bit after all . . .*

A foot missed. Harry shot downwards.

'Harry!'

He heard Billie's voice, cutting through the shrieks of the crowd. His arms flailed, the ball, teaspoon, and the watch were gone, but one hand flung out and grabbed the very bottom of one of the rail's struts, just where it met the edge of the deck. Harry jolted to a halt, a knife of pain twisting in his shoulder muscles as he dangled against the ship's iron panels, his bare feet scrabbling to get a hold. The propellers thundered, his fingers ached, and he knew they wouldn't hold for much longer. But then Billie's hands gripped his arm, and Arthur's too. Their eyes were wide with fear as they hauled him back over the rail, and collapsed with him onto the deck in a heap.

'Sorry about your grandfather's watch, Perkin,' Harry gasped. 'You were right, shouldn't have tried the dance . . .'

Several members of the crowd had fainted. A couple more were running for help, their shoes pounding the deck, and one of the bonneted ladies seemed to be having a hysterical fit. The rest of the crowd were staring, their faces pale. Amidst them all stood Perkin, his mouth hanging open, aghast. Harry sat up, shrugged forlornly and then, deliberately arranging his face in a puzzled expression, peered at Perkin's left jacket pocket.

'Wait a minute,' he muttered. 'What's that?'

Harry stumbled to his feet. He tottered up to Perkin and, performing an even more quizzical frown,

7

pushed his hand into Perkin's pocket. Inside, his wrist flicked, and a familiar shape rolled out of his sleeve. He stepped back, pulled out his hand and, trying to look as mystified as possible, held up the leather ball.

'Well, what do we have here?'

A ball, that was the answer. But Perkin seemed to have forgotten the word for that perfectly ordinary object, because his mouth still hung open, making no sound at all. Harry scratched his head with more puzzlement, and delved into another of the sailor's pockets. Another concealed flick of his wrist, and he drew out the tea-spoon—Perkin wasn't able to say what that was either, and nor could anyone else in the crowd, although they were starting to make other sounds: gasps, mutters, and even a few chuckles. Harry tossed the ball to Arthur, the spoon to Billie, and then pushed right into the insides of Perkin's jacket, towards the pocket by his chest. In amongst the warm cloth, he detected the vibrations of the sailor's heart, beating even faster than his own. He delved into the inside pocket. Another flick of his wrist, another shape slid from his sleeve and, after a couple of other quick movements, he drew out the pocket watch, dangling at the end of its chain.

'Let me check it for sea water,' Harry said, holding it up, and shaking it next to his ear.

'Good idea—salt water can have a nasty effect on a

watch's mechanism if it gets inside,' said Arthur, leaning in with a handkerchief.

Harry gave the watch a couple more shakes, and then wiped it with the handkerchief before handing it back to Perkin. Then he swung round and, as the crowd clapped and cheered and threw even more coins into the buckets, he joined hands with his friends. Together, they performed the move that they had practised more than any other.

A long, slow bow.

'Good old Perkin,' chuckled Arthur, half an hour later, as they stood at the front of the ship. The noise of the engine was quieter, no propellers churning below. All around, the sea chopped and swelled, and land could be seen ahead, a murky grey smear. Harry and his friends watched it grow closer.

'Not a bad trick, that.' Billie was chuckling, too. 'The crowd definitely thought you were done for—you should have seen their faces when you fell.'

'Can't believe you caught the watch *and* the teaspoon *and* the ball as you went down.' Arthur nodded. 'I reckoned you'd drop the spoon at least.'

'Shame we couldn't have got more cash out of it.' Billie stared down at the two buckets by her boots. 'Now Perkin's got his cut, there's not so much.'

'Doesn't matter, we're doing it mainly for the practice, aren't we?' Harry said. 'Eight days at sea—didn't want us getting out of shape.'

'You're right, that wouldn't be good,' Arthur agreed. 'We've got an extremely successful theatre act to keep going, after all.'

'Not to mention a certain other business that might be worth keeping in shape for.' Billie lowered her voice, even though no one was nearby.

Harry's hands were on the ship's rail again, and they tightened. Those flickers and twitches had died down since the trick, but they were back now, and were stronger. *Good, good*—because there was even more reason to concentrate. Glancing across, he saw that Billie was holding the rail tightly too, her knuckles a little pale; further along, Arthur was biting down on his lip. Narrowing his eyes, Harry focused on the land ahead.

'Still haven't got the faintest idea of what this new mission might be. Sending us all the way to England— why?' Billie muttered. 'Although it's better than last time, when we woke out of a drugged sleep stuffed inside locked suitcases, and had to fight our way out.'

'That's just the way the Order of the White Crow works.' Arthur said. 'It's a highly secret crime-solving organization—they tell their members only the bare minimum about anything. Safer that way.'

'Maybe—or maybe they're worried that, if we knew what our next investigation involved, we'd never have boarded this ship,' said Billie. 'Imagine if we'd known what we were getting into, back in New Orleans? The whole business of the Demon Curse, we'd have gone running—'

'No we wouldn't have, and you know that better than anyone.' Harry cut his friend off, but his voice was calm. 'Thanks to us and the Order, New Orleans is a lot safer now.'

Billie nodded. Next to her, Arthur nodded too. They were saying nothing, but Harry knew that they were thinking about unexplained comas, dark magic, a deserted lunatic asylum—the terrifying but spectacular events of their last investigation. And they would be thinking about the mysterious organization they worked for too, and everything they had been told about it. *The overthrow of evil, wherever it may lie . . .* Those were the words that had been muttered to them. Harry focused on the land ahead but, at the same time, a corner of his mouth curved upwards in a smile.

'The Order may not have told us much. But that doesn't mean they've told us nothing at all.' He reached into his jacket. 'Remember the coded note, hidden inside the telephone? Telling us to pack up our theatre act and catch this ship?'

'Ah yes—and telling us where we could pick up more information about the mission, once we docked in England.' Arthur was smiling too.

'A certain mailbox 721, at Southampton Dock.' Billie grinned over her shoulder, glancing back towards the ship's stern. 'A certain mailbox used by a certain able seaman, it turns out.'

'Supposedly so he can receive letters and small parcels meant just for him,' added Arthur, chuckling now. 'Although my guess is, this once, it might contain a little something for us too.'

'Good old Perkin,' said Harry. Inside his jacket, his hand slid into the inside pocket. As it did so, he couldn't help practising that little move one last time, the flash of a hand that had not only rolled Perkin's watch out of his sleeve, but had also lifted a certain other item out of the sailor's inside pocket. Harry drew his hand out, and that item dangled from his fingers, catching the sun. It was a key, and something was etched on it.

Mailbox 721.

Chapter Two

The crowd surged down the gangplank. Harry ducked between the jostling passengers, sliding through. Porters grappled with suitcases, sailors tugged packing trunks but Harry and his friends moved easily, with only a couple of small bags between them, and Billie's ukulele strapped across her back. In a few minutes, they were inside the port buildings, heading for the mailboxes, a collection of locked metal doors with letter-sized openings that lined a nearby wall.

'Reckon I could pick that lock,' said Harry, stopping in front of 721. His fingers delved in his pocket, looking for the little bent nail he always kept there. 'I'd be quick.'

'Not quick enough. We're in a public place, it's broad daylight and we've got a key anyway—honestly, Harry.' Billie took Perkin's key and opened the door. 'Plenty of chances for lock-picking soon, I bet. Now let's see—'

She fished through the box. Inside were various ordinary letters, probably from Perkin's family or maybe a girlfriend. Billie pushed them to one side, and took out another envelope, one that wasn't addressed to Perkin or to anyone at all. But it had a distinctive mark in its bottom left corner: a white crow circled with black. She slit it open, and pulled out four stubs of card.

'Train tickets.' Arthur peered at the stubs. 'For the eleven thirty-eight from here to London—we'd better hurry. And here comes Perkin, anyway.'

The midshipman was halfway across the hall in a flustered state, digging in his pockets, searching for the key. He stopped, and started tearing through his jacket, even pulling out its lining. Hundreds of coins fell out and started rolling across the floor. Scrabbling after them, he didn't notice Harry walking past, and dropping the key into the nearest pocket of the flying-about jacket.

'Easier putting it back in than taking it out,' Harry said to his friends, as they followed the signs to the Southampton Dock train station.

'Ah, Perkin,' said Arthur. 'Don't want him missing out on his letters and stuff.'

'He did deliberately gamble with Harry's life for the sake of a bit of cash,' pointed out Billie.

'Not really a gamble.' Harry shrugged. 'Wasn't really any chance of me slipping, was there?'

'Big-head,' said Billie, but she laughed as the three of them hurried out of the building. And they were all still laughing as they took their seats in a compartment of a railway carriage, on the train to London Waterloo.

'Carriage five, compartment seven, seats one, two, and three,' said Arthur, checking the details on the stubs again, and then holding up the fourth one. 'So who's this other ticket for?'

'Maybe it's for Mr James,' said Billie, swinging round her ukulele and strumming a chord. 'Just like him to turn up unexpectedly.'

Harry checked the spare ticket, and studied the seat opposite him. He frowned, noticing a slight bulge in the cushioning. Over the last year or so, he had studied other magicians endlessly, watching for the tiniest clue in order to discover their secrets, a missing seam in a coat perhaps, or an over-long sleeve, and now here was a clue of a different kind: a bulge in a train seat. *Quite a big clue actually*, he thought, as he leaned close and heard a muffled ringing. He felt around the seat, flipped up the cushion, and pulled out a telephone from underneath, its bell jangling, its wire disappearing into the seat's insides. He gripped its ebony stem, and lifted the earpiece from its cradle.

'Hello?' he said.

'Excuse the usual precautions,' a familiar voice crackled. 'It really is best that we are not seen together—for your safety, and mine too.'

Mr James, like Billie said. Harry closed his eyes and saw that pale suit, that neatly trimmed white beard, that steady gaze. Harry had been balanced on a tightrope high over a Manhattan street the first time he had seen that gentleman, and their encounters since had been equally strange. He gripped the earpiece tighter, but also angled it so that Billie and Arthur, who were leaning close, could hear.

'Where are you then?' Billie peered out through the window at the station.

'I'm nearby,' Mr James said. 'I emphatically do not wish to blow your cover by being seen with you—the whole point of bringing you to England was to get you away from the rumours that were starting to grow around you, thanks to your remarkable achievements. Now, we must keep this conversation short—once the train starts moving, the wire connecting us will snap.' His words gathered speed. 'Welcome to England. The Order is involved in various affairs this side of the Atlantic, but something has turned up just in the last few hours which we feel will be particularly suited to your talents. Billie, if you check the fourth strut of the luggage rack directly above you . . . ?'

Billie sprang up. A couple of seconds later, she bounced back down onto the seat, gripping a tiny rolled-up slip of paper found at the point where the strut met the carriage wall. She unfurled it. It was blank.

'Light-activated invisible ink?' enquired Arthur.

'Indeed,' crackled the voice. 'If you hold it a little closer to the window . . . '

Wisps of smoke were already rising from the paper's surface. Billie held it at arm's length as the plumes thickened and then drifted away, revealing letters one by one, along with that distinctive mark, a white crow in a black circle:

24, Rigby Gardens, London

'Commit the address to memory,' Mr James's voice crackled on. 'Simply head straight there and your work will be clear. Arthur, you should be able to find your way quite easily—it will be interesting for you to be back in London, your home, in so far as you have ever had one.' The voice quietened. 'Dragged from Paris, then to Berlin, then to New York by that father of yours, a sorry affair. But then all three of you have had fairly troubled beginnings, wouldn't you say?'

Arthur started back from the phone. That tiny line had crinkled on his forehead, the way it did whenever the subject of his father, Lord Dale-Roberts, was raised. Harry exchanged glances with Billie, and thought back to the first time he had met their friend, that nervous-looking boy left to his own devices in an expensive New York apartment. *But why's Mr James bringing all that up now?*

'Arthur, ignored by a father interested only in working for the world's most important banks. Billie, orphaned at an early age, and forced to travel the length of America with just her wits and skilful uku-lele-playing to help her,' said Mr James. 'And then there's you, Harry, with perhaps the most difficult beginnings of all—'

Harry's grip on the earpiece tightened. He listened to the words intently, picking them out from the buzzes of static.

'Brought up in a Budapest slum, only for your family to scatter under mysterious circumstances no one understands. Ending up alone on a run-down ship to America, then struggling to survive those first terrible months in New York by trying to earn a living as a shoe-shiner—great hardship indeed! But it's what happened next that matters—just as with your friends.' Suddenly, the crackly voice had a theatrical tone. 'Three young investigators, all with troubled beginnings. Out of those troubled beginnings, their skills have been forged, and their peculiar determination too, a determination to come to the aid of others, to help those in need. That determination has been tested in New York and in New Orleans, and now it will be tested in London. And I must say, flicking through the file I have in my hands now, I really can't imagine a case more suitable for the three of you.' A rustle of papers, and a chuckle. '*The rescue of others is a triumph for all*—why, that could be your own motto, could it not . . .'

The telephone went dead. A steam whistle had shrieked, the train was rolling forward, and somewhere along its length the telephone's wire must have snapped, as Mr James had warned. Harry held the telephone for a little longer, uncertain what to do with such an expensive piece of machinery, and then stuffed it back under the seat where he had found it. The train rolled on, sliding past the porters and luggage trolleys on the station platform, and Harry's brow furrowed, as he thought back over what Mr James had said.

'Whoah, that's some invisible ink.'

Billie was frowning too, but she was also flinging away the piece of paper, which was no longer smoking, but had burst into flames instead. Harry caught a last glimpse of that address as the paper turned into a curled wisp, the shape of a black fist, or maybe a skull. It floated down to the floor and crumbled into a powdery ash, which floated away over the floorboards.

'Nice touch.' Arthur raised an eyebrow. 'Definitely top secret now—doesn't even exist.'

'But we remember it, don't we? Twenty-three Rigby Gardens—or was it twenty-four?' Billie said. 'I'd write it down somewhere, but it hardly seems fair, the trouble they went to with a self-destructing note.'

'It was twenty-four—don't worry, I'll remember,' said Harry, sitting back in his seat as the train gathered speed. The address was so ordinary-sounding and yet, glancing down, he saw that his fingers had started flexing, performing intricate manoeuvres, practising for whatever might lie ahead. He could feel his heart too, its beat gathering speed with the train, and those flickering sensations crept over his body again, as he wondered what exactly this investigation might be, and then puzzled over Mr James's words again. *The rescue of others is a triumph for all—why, that could be your motto, could it not . . .*

His hands stopped moving. He had seen something on the platform ahead.

'Harry?' Billie looked at him. 'What's up?'

'It can't be anything out there.' Arthur peered through the glass, as a chestnut stall and a luggage trolley flew past. 'We're only just leaving Southampton—nowhere near London yet.'

'But news reaches Southampton of what's *happened* in London, doesn't it?' Harry pointed out through the window at the blurring-past platform. 'Look—'

A man stood near the end of the platform, selling newspapers to a small crowd by a gate. The train raced by and Harry's friends saw him only for a flash, but that was enough to see the headline blazing across the newspapers' front pages. They saw it, every word of it, and the five exclamation marks at the end of it:

MURDER AT 24 RIGBY GARDENS!!!!!

Chapter Three

Harry stepped out of Charing Cross Station. Steam from the trains lingered in his clothes, and he breathed in the odours of the London street, of horses, of pies from a nearby stall, of vegetables being sold in the nearby market. Billie marched up beside him, her ukulele across her back again, and they waited while Arthur hurried towards them with an armful of newspapers.

'I bought them all—*The Times, Daily Chronicle, Telegraph*, everything. They all cover it in their late morning editions.' Arthur flicked through the papers as they walked along the street. 'Try *The Times.*'

He handed Harry a newspaper. Harry read it, Billie peering over his shoulder, as they carried on walking along.

SILENT ASSASSIN!

Dame Flora Cusp, forty-one years of age, was discovered dead this morning at her London home, an apartment at 24 Rigby Gardens. Death is reported to be by gunshot wound although, remarkably, no sound of gunfire was heard during the night. Police officers, under the command of Inspector Horace Newton, are investigating the dark work of this silent assassin, and ask the public to refrain from sensation and rumour. Lady Flora was renowned for her many charitable ventures, in particular for setting up hospitals, most recently in the troubled republic of Ravelstan to help victims of the war there. She was a prominent member of the much-respected charitable society the Benevolent Orphans.

'That's it?' Harry flicked over the page, and back again.

'Yes, and the others just say the same thing.' Arthur tucked the newspapers under his arm, and led his friends across a bridge. 'There'll be a bit more in the afternoon and evening editions, maybe—I'll buy those.'

'Death by gunshot wound.' Billie shook her head. 'Looks like our investigation in London's going to be every bit as nasty as the one in New Orleans, and the one in New York.'

'Oh yes, plenty of nasty stuff goes on in London.'

Arthur stopped briefly on the bridge, and stared out across the city, dark buildings huddled in the grey smog. 'Don't be taken in by all the fancy architecture and reputation for politeness—some of the world's greatest crimes have been committed here: poisonings, assassinations, awful plots, political intrigues—'

'How far is it, Artie?' Harry interrupted. Arthur's knowledge about almost every possible subject was always useful, but it was important not to get distracted.

'Oh yes—sorry. About five minutes from here. Come on.'

He led them over the bridge, and then swung off to the west. They crossed various roads, passed more looming buildings, and then crossed into a park, which seemed pleasant and peaceful enough, despite what Arthur had said. They left through a tall gate, dodged across a busy road, and turned onto a quieter street, lined with trees. Harry saw its sign bolted onto a wall: Rigby Gardens. The street was empty of traffic, and the buildings were white, with iron railings along their fronts, and flower boxes at their windows. Harry and his friends walked down the pavement towards number twenty-four.

It was roped off by policemen, who held back a crowd of journalists from its steps. The journalists were pushing and shoving, waving their notebooks, and

Harry tried to hear what they were saying, but all their questions were shouted at once, and the policemen were shouting, too. Harry walked to the crowd's edge and pushed into it, hoping to catch sight of the journalists' notebooks, but just then everyone fell silent. A senior policeman had emerged at the top of the steps, surveying the journalists with an unfriendly gaze.

'No further information will be given at this time.' His voice was gruff and heavy. 'This investigation proceeds, and I insist that the gentlemen of the press respect that. *Insist*—is that clear?'

He was about fifty years old, sturdily built, with a mutton-chop beard, dark sideburns curling down the edges of his powerful jaw. His uniform was immaculate, its steel buttons gleaming in the light, and his eyes gleamed too, in the darkness beneath his hat's brim. Slowly, those eyes studied each journalist in turn, seeming to gather every bit as much knowledge as any of them might have written in their notebooks.

'Inspector Newton—' One of the journalists spoke up, his voice strangely high. 'Can you at least confirm that the murder occurred at six in the morning— when the owner of the flat below heard a thud, and a scream?'

'I confirm nothing,' the policeman said.

'What can you tell us about the fact that no one was

seen leaving Dame Flora's house after that?' another journalist ventured. 'Not by the door anyway—the owner of the flat below was hammering on it until your men arrived.'

'I make no comment.' Newton's beard twitched, his eyes narrowed, and the journalist who had spoken shuffled back.

'And what of the fact that a gun was fired, yet with no noise?' A journalist near Harry spoke with his hand half over his mouth, hoping not to be seen, but Newton swung towards him anyway.

'No comment, apart from to say what I said at first—that this investigation proceeds, conducted by my men and no one else. Any interference will be dealt with by law.'

No more questions. Instead, the journalists just muttered to each other, but even that displeased Inspector Newton, who glared at them a little longer, and then started talking to his officers, who had gathered around him. Harry watched him from the crowd's edge.

'Can you work out what he's saying, Billie? With the Sherman Jones lip-reading trick?' he whispered. Sherman Jones was a tramp Billie had travelled with for a few weeks on her way up America, and the various skills he had passed onto her had helped them numerous times.

'I'm trying.' Billie squinted. 'But the other police-men keep getting in the way, and that beard round his mouth doesn't help either; Sherman always warned me about beards and over-sized sideburns wrecking a perfectly good lip-read. Anyway, we didn't need lip-reading or any trick at all to hear the first stuff he said. *My men and no one else*—I guess that doesn't include three kids who've just stepped off a ship from New Orleans?'

'You guess right,' said Arthur. 'I suppose it's rea-sonable, what he's saying. If there's been a murder, the police should be left to investigate it—that's their job.'

'The Order of the White Crow don't think so,' said Harry. 'They told us to come here.'

'"Especially suited to your talents", that's what Mr James said—and they must have decided that pretty fast,' Billie said. 'The murder happened at six in the morning, and Mr James put us on the mission just a couple of hours later, down in Southampton. It's really important to them—why?'

'Makes sense to me; sounds exactly like a White Crow mission,' said Harry. He turned away from the crowd and headed out into the street. 'This Dame Flora was giving money to charities, setting up hos-pitals—and she was a member of a charitable society too . . . what was its name?'

'The Benevolent Orphans,' said Arthur, following Harry.

'So a good person, who spent her money on doing good, and now someone's murdered her—that must be Dame Flora's apartment, look.'

Harry had reached the middle of the cobbled street, and was pointing upwards. He had spotted movements in a window five stories up. He watched the shadows, and made out the shapes of policemen's hats, the glimmer of braid on their uniforms. He kept staring, but the window was too high, the angle up from the street too sharp, so he backed across the cobbles a little further, trying to peer up, shading his eyes from the sun—

'What are you doing, boy?'

The steely eyes were even more penetrating up close. Inspector Newton was standing right over Harry and his friends, his heavy arms folded, his bearded jaw set, several officers gathered behind him. Harry opened his mouth, but no words came out; fortunately there were plenty coming from Billie.

'There's no need to worry, officer. We were just walking through, taking a short-cut on our way to—'

'Just walking? Didn't look like that to me.' Newton kept his eyes on Harry for a while longer. Then he moved them across to Billie. 'Standing around, peering up at windows. That's what I observed.'

'Can't blame us for getting interested.' Billie tried something different. 'Wandering through, trying to see what's going on, no harm in it—'

'But possibly some money in it. Are you in the pay of one of these gentlemen of the press perhaps, helping them gather the information they so desire?' Newton glanced across at the journalists again, and then straight back at Billie. 'Interfering with a police investigation is a crime. A serious one, particularly if done for financial gain.'

'We're just lost actually—' A few splutters from Billie, but that was all.

'I'm talking.' The steely eyes silenced her. 'And I'm telling you to get on your way. Now.'

Harry was already walking. Arthur hurried beside him, blushing, and Billie tagged after them, her lips silently moving as she kept trying to think up things to say. Suddenly, Harry grabbed his friends and tugged them both behind a tree. He put a finger to Billie's lips and squeezed Arthur's shoulder reassuringly. Then he edged his head back around the tree, peering down the street.

Harry watched Newton and the officers cross to the other side of the road. Ahead of them, two policemen were waiting by the doorway to the building directly opposite 24 Rigby Gardens. When Newton arrived,

Harry saw one of the men point upwards. But immediately Newton grabbed his sleeve and held it down. Harry watched those eyes do their work on the officer, whose head lowered, whose shoulders sunk. Newton said a few words before releasing the officer's arm, and disappeared into the building.

'That block of flats—it's directly across from number twenty-four.' Arthur was peering around the tree too.

'Maybe they think the shot came from the building opposite?' Billie said. 'That would explain why no one was seen leaving the flat afterwards.'

'Doesn't explain why no one heard a shot, though,' Arthur mused. 'Lots of people have been trying to invent a gun that fires with no noise, but no one's managed it yet, as far as I know. And if this assassin shot her while she was inside her flat, how come none of the windows are broken? The bullet would have had to smash through them, unless they were open, and they wouldn't be on a cold October morning . . . '

'They're up on the roof, look,' said Harry, pointing up at the new building.

He could see policemen's hats bobbing in and out of view. Voices echoed down from the flat roof, seven storeys high. Some sort of search was being conducted up there, and that was where Newton would be heading. Harry swung back to the journalists, who were still milling around the doorway to number twenty-four. They had been so busy asking questions, so busy scribbling in their notebooks, that they had failed to spot that something was happening only a short distance away, up on the roof of the building opposite.

But what, exactly?

Harry stepped out into the street. He walked down to an alleyway, and spotted a fire-escape running up the side of the building into which Newton had disappeared. It led all the way up to the roof, but there was a gate at the bottom. He and his friends ran up to it. It was locked but his fingers were already in his pocket, fishing out that little bent nail.

'Told you it wouldn't be long till you got the chance to use it.' Billie examined the lock. 'Nice and dark here too, not like doing it in full view of the port authority—'

Harry's bent nail slotted between the lock's levers, prising them apart. The gate swung open and shut after him and his friends. Their boots chimed up the metal stairs, and a few seconds later they were at the top, swinging over a shallow wall onto the flat roof. Immediately, Harry grabbed his friends again and pulled them behind a chimney stack, because he had spotted several policemen on the roof's far side, gathered around a large pair of open hatches. *Waiting for*

Newton, he thought, and he huddled against the chimney's brickwork, crammed next to his friends. They had gone completely still.

'There she is, Harry . . . '

Harry turned to see Billie and Arthur, frozen. They had a clear view across the street to Dame Flora's apartment. Harry looked, and froze like his friends. There was something a little way back from the window.

A wheeled trolley with a blanket-draped body on it.

'Dame Flora,' Arthur whispered.

The shape beneath the blanket was unmistakable: the rise and fall of a head, a chest, the body's lower half. About halfway along the trolley, the blanket had caught on something and its edge was lifted, revealing darkness underneath. Within that darkness, the pale shape of a hand. It was white, almost as white as the frilled sleeve that surrounded its wrist. Harry flinched, but kept looking.

'Horrible,' Arthur said. 'Shot down in her own home.'

'It could easily have been done from here,' Billie said. 'If we can see into her flat, then so could whoever did this.'

'But what about the windows?' Harry whispered. 'They're not broken, so they must have been open— but why would they be?'

'The flowerbox,' said Arthur.

Arthur was leaning forward and looking below the window, where a particularly neatly tended box of flowers could be seen. A small ornamental watering can lay amongst them, as if it had been dropped. Arthur took out a leather notebook from his pocket, and quickly sketched the scene with a pen, taking care over the exact shape of the flowers.

'Japanese chrysanthemums, I think—I'll check later,' he said. 'They're not easy to look after, I've heard. Need constant care, particularly in October. What if every morning Dame Flora opened that window and watered them? Maybe whoever did this knew about that routine. What if they were up here at that exact moment, waiting for the window sash to lift up and then ... '

Something caught Harry's eye a short distance away across the roof they were on. More police ropes surrounded a small area near the edge, just a blank bit of the roof's grey surface, as far as he could see.

And three tiny shapes, right in the middle.

'Back soon.'

Harry slid away from his friends, darting to the next chimney stack, a little closer to the roped-off space. Edging around it, he saw the policemen by the hatch snap to attention as Inspector Newton arrived on the roof. Immediately they started answering their superior's questions, pointing towards the roped-off space, and then gathering tightly around him, listening to his muttered instructions. Harry took the opportunity to dart to the next chimney stack, even closer to the ropes, and whatever they surrounded.

Bullet casings. Crouched behind the chimney, Harry could see them: three little metal tubes, one standing upright, two lying on their side. The policemen had drawn little chalk circles around each of them. Leaning forward, he studied the circular metal base of one of casings, which was half-angled towards him. It seemed to have some letters engraved into it, in a circle round its edge. 'M', that was the first one, and Harry tried to decipher the others, but he was too far away, and the base wasn't facing him directly enough. Narrowing his eyes, he leaned out even further.

'Remain where you are, gentlemen. I shall inspect this myself.'

Newton was crossing the roof. Harry scrambled back behind the chimney. He glanced towards where Billie and Arthur were hiding, and saw that they had drawn back too. *Good.* He stayed where he was, his shoulders against the brickwork, listening to the policeman's shoes as they trod heavily across the roof, and stopped. For some time, he heard nothing at all. He peered round the chimney again.

Newton was knelt down by the ropes. That bearded face was lowered, but the tiniest movement might mean he was staring straight at Harry, just a few yards away. Still, that was unlikely, because Newton appeared entirely absorbed with what he had found; he was picking up the three bullet casings, examining them in his palm. Harry watched the little gleaming shapes, slightly closer to him now. One of them rotated in the policeman's fingers, and its round base caught the light; Harry tried to decipher the letters again, but he was still too far away.

Unlike Newton. The inspector was angling one of the casings so that its base was just a few inches from his eyes. Harry watched him, and noticed how Newton glanced quickly over his shoulder towards the policemen by the hatch and then back to the bullet casing.

Newton folded the casings into a pale handkerchief and shoved them into his pocket. With a bulky thumb, the policeman rubbed out the little chalk circles on the roof, leaving no trace behind. Only when that was done did he stand and head back towards the other officers.

Harry stayed where he was. He listened to the tread of Newton's shoes, fading away. He waited, and then risked another peer around the chimney towards the hatch. Newton was marching straight past the other policemen without a word, and descending into the hatch.

Chapter Four

'A circle of letters?' asked Arthur. 'Can you tell us anything more, Harry? As in—anything at all?'

Harry and his friends rattled along in a horse-drawn cab. Arthur had gathered several more newspapers, the afternoon editions he had mentioned, and he was riffling through them, searching for more information. But clearly he hadn't found anything useful, because he kept snapping whichever paper he was reading shut, and asking the same thing.

'The tiniest detail, Harry? Apart from the first letter being "M"? And the circle of letters being, well . . . circular?'

'I'm sorry. If I'd managed to get a bit closer. Or look at it a bit longer . . .'

'I could start researching it, you see. Track down where the bullets were made, maybe. It's our only clue.'

'Except it's not *our* clue at all,' Billie interrupted, also reading a newspaper. 'It's Inspector Newton's clue, and it's nice and safe in his pocket, not seen by Harry or anyone else.'

'He is in charge of the investigation, remember.' Arthur flicked through another newspaper, as grey London buildings travelled past the window. 'As for telling us to clear off earlier—that's not necessarily suspicious either. We're just kids, as far as he's concerned.'

'True, can't expect him to figure out we're also kids who work for a highly secret crime-solving organization,' said Harry. 'It's highly secret, that's the whole point.'

'That's right, and if he thought we were just kids, he'd have every reason for telling us to stay away,' Arthur added. 'Given what we saw.'

'I know—poor Dame Flora.' Billie shuddered. 'Such a good person, too—the newspapers all say that.'

'Yes, it's about the only thing they agree on, actually.' Arthur looked back at his newspaper and tutted. 'Honestly, I know Newton's clamped down on information, but that's no reason for what these journalists have done—they've just started inventing stuff, different things in every paper. But you're right, they're all completely in tune about what a good sort Dame Flora was, a saintly sort even, and the same goes for this Benevolent Orphans charity. Talking of which, it looks like we're here—it's the St Pancras Hotel, look.'

The cab wheeled to a halt, across the street from a large pillared building with stone steps leading to doors of glass and bronze. Harry jumped down from the cab with Billie, while Arthur paid the driver. Two uniformed men waited by the hotel's doors, waving through the many journalists who were hurrying up the steps. Harry recognized a few from Rigby Gardens, but there were several others, some clutching notebooks and pencils, others carrying little portable desks under their arms.

'Will we be allowed in?' Harry crossed the street, eyeing the doormen suspiciously.

'I think so. It's a public event, according to this notice.' Arthur held up one of the newspapers, and read. '"At four o'clock this afternoon, the Benevolent Orphans will make a statement about the recent demise of their beloved fellow member, Dame Flora Cusp." Obviously, we don't want to draw attention to ourselves, but we can simply turn up, I think.'

Billie and Arthur headed up the steps. Harry was about to follow them, but then looked back towards the horse-drawn cab, which was still waiting across the street. He had noticed something out of the corner of his eye—a man, talking to the driver.

He had slid out of the crowd, and jumped up on the

cab's footplate. His back was turned, his body covered by a dark cape. *Another customer, giving directions about where he wished to go,* Harry thought. But the conversation was going on for some time, and the driver kept looking up in the direction of Harry and his friends. He was even pointing at them as he carried on talking. Harry trod back down the steps, trying to make the figure out more closely.

But he was too late. The cape fluttered, the figure jumped down from the footplate, and darted towards an alleyway a little further down the street. Ducking into it, the man turned, and stared directly at Harry, but the alley was too dark for Harry to make out his face properly—only the outline of it, bulkily misshapen on one side.

Harry jumped down the steps, trying to see more. But carts rattled past, crowds pushed and shoved. Harry glanced up and down the street, looking for the quickest way across.

And when he looked back at the alleyway, the figure had drawn back into the darkness completely, and disappeared.

Harry and his friends took their seats in the hotel conference hall. Rows of velvet-cushioned chairs had been set out in front of a stage, on which a long table stood

with four cards positioned along it, each one display-
ing a neatly written name. *Lord Jaspar. Lady Brewster.
Sir Julian Elkins-Ford. Professor Roger Winterskill.* Harry
glanced at each one, memorizing it. All around journalists waited, jotting in their notepads or opening
their portable desks.

'With luck, they'll actually get told something
this time.' Arthur studied the journalists in an unim-
pressed way. 'I just hope they get it right when they
submit their copy.'

'It's true, there really are lot of mistakes in these
papers.' Billy was still checking hers. 'This one here—
whoever wrote this hasn't even got the address of this
press conference right, says it's at the Grosvenor Hotel,
not St Pancras.' She looked around. 'Maybe he's waiting there now?'

'You can't really blame them,' Arthur said. 'When
there's a big story like this, they're so desperate to sell
newspapers that they'll write any old thing. And people are so desperate to read it, they don't particularly
notice if it's completely right or not.' He took out his
own notebook. 'Here we go, anyway.'

Behind the table on the stage a door had opened,
and the four Benevolent Orphans filed out. The
first was a lady, festooned with jewellery, and she was
closely followed by two middle-aged gentlemen—a

straggly-haired one with a pink-tinted monocle in his left eye and a tall, thin one wearing an expensive suit with several silk handkerchiefs protruding from its pockets. Their faces strained, they each took their place behind their name stand and waited for the fourth Benevolent Orphan, the most strained-looking of all. Frail and elderly, he tottered in with the help of an ivory-handled walking cane, his body hunched, his face dominated by two dark sunken eyes. The other Benevolent Orphans helped the old man, taking his arms, guiding him to his chair, and at last he sunk weakly into place behind his name card: *Lord Jaspar*.

'Welcome to you all. Never before, in the history of this society that I lead, have we met in such tragic circumstances.' Tears gleamed in the darkness of the old man's eyes. 'The threat facing us is profound and—'

'Tell us about Dame Flora! Not you!' interrupted a journalist.

'The Rigby Gardens murder—that's what we want to know about!' shouted another.

'Have the police told you anything? Tell us!' Another voice from the back.

The journalists waved their notepads, their shouts blotting out Lord Jaspar's feeble tones. The velvet-suited gentleman next to him, Sir Julian Elkins-Ford, offered him a handkerchief with polka dots to dab at his eyes, and Lady Brewster offered him a bottle of smelling salts, which he held to his nose. Further along, Professor Winterskill, the gentleman with the pink-tinted monocle, staggered up and tried to silence the rabble.

'Our noble leader *is* talking about Dame Flora! If you would only listen!' he exclaimed, gripping the lapels of his jacket with shaking hands. 'To speak of the Benevolent Orphans is the *same thing* as to speak of Dame Flora—our society was her life, just as it is for each and every one of us.'

'Indeed!' Lady Brewster retrieved her smelling salts from Lord Jaspar, took a lengthy draught herself, and sobbed. 'Look into the hearts of every one of us, and you shall see the words "Benevolent Orphans" written there. Along with our motto: *the rescue of others is a triumph for all!'*

The journalists listened. Possibly their throats were sore from shouting; perhaps they had realized that there was little point in calling out questions if they couldn't hear any answers. Whatever the reason, the gentlemen of the press fell silent, as Lady Brewster's words echoed in Harry's thoughts. *The rescue of others is a triumph for all.* Harry closed his eyes. He remembered those same words, said by a different voice, crackling down a telephone line in a train carriage. *Why, that could be your own motto, could it not . . .*

'The Benevolent Orphans—we are exactly what our society's name suggests.' Lord Jaspar sat forward, his face pale, the hand that had gripped his cane now clutching his other arm instead, with a curious tightness. 'Each one of us was cruelly orphaned as a child and suffered during our most tender years as a result. Through hard work and good fortune, we have gone on to prosper, to grow wealthy and even influential—but we have never forgotten those sad beginnings! And we have therefore vowed to give as much as we can of our wealth to those in need, to those who, as we once used to be, are vulnerable and weak. Because, as our motto says, *the rescue of others . . .*'

'*. . . is a triumph for all!* So true!' Sir Julian Elkins-Ford dabbed at his own eyes with a different handkerchief, a flower-patterned one this time, plucked from another pocket of his expensive suit. 'My fortune was made with a shipping business, as you gentlemen probably know—but I have never forgotten my early days, toiling in the London docks. My fortune is therefore devoted to children such as I was—through the creation of the Benevolent Orphans schools for the poor, set up all over our land.'

'My career will be familiar to you too,' interrupted Lady Brewster, adjusting her jewellery and tapping her name plate with a finger. 'My romantic novels are hugely popular; they have led to the establishment of an entire publishing empire. But I have never forgotten my miserable orphanage childhood, and so I devote every penny that I can to the Benevolent Orphans libraries, which are being constructed in the poorest districts of our nation's cities.'

'All of us, in our different ways, further the society's work,' said Lord Jaspar, and he gestured at Professor Winterskill. 'My good friend Winterskill uses the proceeds from his international law company to ensure safe working conditions at factories, while I myself devote my wealth, made from various business enterprises, to funding medicines for the poor, providing assistance for the deaf, financing hygienic freshwater delivery systems, and, most recently, campaigning for world peace.' His hand returned to his arm, and clutched it harder. 'Like all of us, I hope to make some good from my sorry orphan past. But who was more successful at that than dear Dame Flora Cusp?'

'Her wealth came from sheer chance!' Lady Brewster said. 'Her childhood was spent in misery, after her missionary parents lost their lives to illness, and she told me many times of the blessed day when the news arrived of an unexpected inheritance, plucking her from poverty. *Why should only I be so fortunate?* she said—and she devoted her life from then on to helping others. Already trained as a nurse, she set up hospitals all over the world, and not just any hospitals— ones in the places they're needed most. Countries tormented by disease or flood, for example—and most recently one in the tragic country of Ravelstan, so terribly afflicted by war . . .'

The journalists scribbled away. Some of them were writing with care now, and Harry saw the words 'Ravelstan' and 'war' curling from pen nibs all around him. He felt a tapping on his arm, and turned to see Arthur, beckoning him and Billie to draw near.

'Sorry, I should have explained about Ravelstan earlier,' he said. 'It's a small country near Russia—well, it should be two countries really, and that's the point. The poor people of West Ravelstan want to break away, but the king of Ravelstan won't let them, so he's waging an awful war to stop that happening. Terrible battles, lots of people killed, horrible—'

'A noble lady!' Up on the stage, Professor Winterskill tugged the pink monocle from his eye, wiped it clean of tears, and squashed it back in. 'Cast your gaze upon her picture—see for yourselves what a creature of kindness she was!'

He pulled at a little rope, behind him on the wall. A pulley squeaked, and a cloth fluttered off a painting standing on an easel, on the far left of the stage.

Depicted in the painting was a middle-aged lady with a simple bonnet and neat grey hair, with the gentlest of expressions on her face, large brown eyes shining from the oils. But Harry looked away, and saw Billie and Arthur do the same—he knew why. *That pale lifeless hand.* Harry winced at the memory, made even more horrible as Dame Flora gazed so warmly out of the painting.

'A gentle soul!' Lord Jaspar wheezed. 'And yet determined, too. Nothing could stop dear Dame Flora as she went about her work, not even the many dangers she faced setting up hospitals in such troubled places. To think that this gentle soul should suffer a hideous death by cold-blooded murder—'

'His arm! Look what's happening to his arm!'

A journalist to Harry's left yelled out. He was pointing with his pen, straight at the old man in the wheelchair, and a blob of ink flew from his pen's nib and landed on a chair, soaking into the velvet. But Harry's gaze was fixed on a far more sinister stain, the one spreading on the cloth of Lord Jaspar's jacket. The old man gripped it, and his fingers shone red when he lifted them away. His fellow society members sorrowfully lowered their heads.

'Ah—you are most observant, as I would expect of your profession,' Lord Jaspar gasped. 'You bring me to the second announcement of the day. I am afraid that Dame Flora, although she paid the ultimate price, was not alone in suffering an attack. I have just returned from Paris, where I was busy arranging my latest peace conference—an attempt to stop the war in Ravelstan, actually, something I have been working on with Dame Flora. And it was there, in Paris, that I too nearly fell victim to this silent assassin five days ago!'

There was more than one blot of ink flying now. The journalists' pens were darting in and out of their wells, and stray spatters arched everywhere. More questions were cried out, while up on stage the Benevolent Orphans helped Lord Jaspar, handing him a glass of water, offering extra cushions for his chair. But the old man, even as his blood spread, seemed energized by a desperate vigour.

'I had just successfully arranged the conference when it happened. I was walking back to my hotel late at night when the shot was fired. No sound, but I saw sparks as it ricocheted off a nearby wall. I saw a caped figure up at the window aiming a rifle at me. I stumbled away, but not before another shot had been fired, shattering my arm, leaving me with a wound that re-opens at times of distress, no matter how tightly it is bandaged—'

'Why did we not learn of this before?' a journalist shouted. 'A week ago, you said this happened?'

'I hoped to keep it secret for the sake of our society! We spend our own fortunes, but we also seek contributions from others; what would be the effect if word got out that, as well as undertaking acts of charity, we Benevolent Orphans are also the subjects of assassination attempts?' Lord Jaspar stared at his fellow members. 'But now that Dame Flora has suffered her fate, it is out in the open! Best make a clean breast of it! Better let the world know of the peril our society finds itself in!'

'Grave peril!' Sir Julian cried, dabbing his forehead with yet another handkerchief, this one with Chinese dragons on it. 'This silent assassin has murdered one of us, and made a deadly attempt on another! Who can know his motive—possibly one of our charitable endeavours has offended some powerful interest? If so, then we are all at risk, because he will most certainly go on to kill every last one of us—'

'Why?' The words jumped out of Harry's mouth, and he jumped up from his chair. He had been sat there silently for too long, and he hadn't been able to stop himself. The journalists around him muttered, noticing him and his young friends for the first time. *So much for keeping up our cover.*

'*Why*, young man? Why is our society in peril?' Professor Winterskill stared at him, and tried to brush his straggly hair from his face, but it clung there, damp with perspiration. 'Because it *is* a society! We are bound together, my fellow Orphans—bound by a solemn vow!'.

'Each one of us has sworn that, if any of us dies, we shall continue his or her work for evermore!' Sir Julian cried. 'We are looking through Dame Flora's papers even now, to make sure we shall do so for her. If Lord Jaspar were to have been killed, we would be looking through his papers, too. Any powerful interest that seeks to stop some charitable act of theirs—they will not achieve their purpose until every last one of us is dead!'

'*The rescue of others is a triumph for all*—there is no nobler cry.' With great effort, Lord Jaspar rose from his chair. 'But for how long will that cry be heard if a brutal assassin is on the loose, hunting us down, each and every one of us?'

He collapsed into his chair with such force that it nearly fell back from the table. Lady Brewster held it still, but Lord Jaspar sprawled wildly, blood still spreading on his arm. The Benevolent Orphans gathered around him, hoisting him up and carrying him away, and the journalists dashed away too, slamming shut their portable desks, tucking away their notebooks and racing for the door. Chairs tipped up, shoes skidded over the hotel lobby's marble floor, the revolving doors leading to the street outside spun and flashed. And then they were gone, and so were the Orphans, leaving only the tipped-over chairs, a few confused members of the hotel staff, the deserted table and name cards, and Harry and his friends.

Harry stood up. He walked slowly towards the table where the Orphans had sat. Behind him, he heard Billie and Arthur, muttering.

'Deadlines.' Arthur was looking out into the lobby, and at the still-spinning hotel doors. 'They'll all want to make sure their newspaper's first on the street with all this information.'

'Let's hope they get a few of the details right this time,' said Billie.

'They don't care,' said Arthur, making a note of his own in his book. 'People want to follow a good story, and they know that. They'll just make sure it's as thrilling as possible.' His grip tightened on his pen. 'It's not like they've got to actually do anything about it.'

'Good point—one thing to write about something, another to find out what's at the bottom of it.' Billie drummed her fingers on the back of a chair. 'An assassin on the loose, a murder, an attempted murder, a society that's devoted to nothing but good—I can definitely see why the Order of the White Crow want to get involved.'

'Yes—if there's one thing worth protecting, it's a charitable society.' Arthur looked back up at the table. 'Particularly one as committed as this one.'

Harry placed his hands on the table. Those flickering sensations travelled up from his fingertips into his arms, spreading all over his body, and the feelings quickened the longer he stood there, looking at the different name cards, recalling what the gentle, eccentric people sat behind them had said. His gaze moved left and took in the kindly eyes of Dame Flora, staring out of the painting. *The rescue of others is a triumph for all...*

Mr James. Harry closed his eyes, and remembered the telephone conversation, every static-surrounded scrap of it. *Three young investigators, all with troubled beginnings. Out of those troubled beginnings, their skills have been forged, and their peculiar determination too.* Mr James had mentioned holding the investigation file in his hand—he must have known that, just a few hours later, those investigators would be bumping into a society of noble, well-meaning people who also spoke of troubled beginnings and of a desire to help. *The rescue of others*—Harry muttered that motto to himself once again. It was a bit old fashioned, a bit English, but otherwise Mr James was right, perhaps it really could be a motto for him and his friends . . .

'Harry?' Arthur was waving at him. 'I think we should find somewhere to stay. A hotel, perhaps? It's getting dark.'

Harry glanced out through a window. Light was fading from the London sky, and the buildings looked even gloomier. Briefly, he thought about Arthur's suggestion. *A hotel.* But then he looked down at his fingertips, which were still resting on the table, and still alive with those flickers and twitches. *Seems a shame to waste the energy,* he thought. *And maybe it's best to keep on practising—for what lies ahead.*

'I've got a better idea for where to stay, Artie,' he said. 'Not sure how much rest we'll get, though.'

Chapter Five

The curtain rose, the tassels along its bottom edge fluttering. Pulleys rattled as the stagehands hauled at ropes, and the higher they winched the curtain, the louder the audience's roar became, no longer muffled by the wall of cloth. Harry felt the noise billow around him as he stood on the spot, and performed a quick bow. Then he walked forward to what was waiting for him at the front of the stage.

A chair, with various coils of rope neatly stacked around it. Arthur was hurrying in from the wings with a couple more coils, and he dumped them with the others as Harry sat down.

'So not exactly a hotel then,' Arthur muttered in his ear.

'It's quite a comfy dressing room they're offering us,' Harry said. 'We'll get a good night's sleep in the end, don't you worry. Plus there's a fee and they're throwing in an evening meal. They've just told me that—'

'Hang on, I've got to say the next bit.' Arthur swung round to the audience, puffed out his chest, and shouted as loud as he could with his reedy voice. 'Behold Harry, the boy who cannot be trapped, cannot be contained! Harry Houdini, they call him, and his abilities to escape defy explanation! Magic dwells within him, they say, and you shall witness that tonight, with your very eyes! Friend Billie, do we have our volunteers?'

'We do, we do!' Billie was far back in the auditorium, hurrying down the aisle, beckoning several members of the audience from their seats, all strong-looking men. Harry concentrated on his breathing, keeping it steady, as Billie led the men up a little ladder at the front of the stage, and then across the wooden boards. Their heavy bodies surrounded him, and a few of them picked up the ropes as Arthur's speech continued.

'To work you go, gentlemen! Tie him as tightly as you can! He is a mere boy, but imagine he is the most dangerous of criminals, the most violent of men. Tie him so he cannot escape. Do your worst, gentlemen!'

They're taking him seriously, thought Harry, wincing as the first rope pulled tight around his chest. He gritted his teeth, beads of perspiration forming on his forehead. Another rope looped around his arm, three more circled his ankles, and his body shook as those ropes pulled tight too. Peering down, Harry concentrated on the knots being tied all over him. He recognized most of them, but there were a few unfamiliar ones, knots popular in England perhaps, and he studied those with care, watching the ends of rope as they looped and twisted.

'Finished, gentlemen? Have you done your worst, as I requested?'

A final knot snapped tight around Harry's ankles. The men stepped back, brushing fibres of rope from their hands, and headed across the stage towards their seats. Dribbles of sweat drained down the sides of Harry's face, and his whole body ached as the knots, hard as fists, dug into his skin. Beside him, Billie waved down another rope, which was being lowered from high above the stage. An iron hook dangled from it, and Billie curved it under the ropes by Harry's feet.

'Let the escape begin!'

Harry was upside-down. The rope with the hook was winched upwards again, tugging him up off the chair, ankles first. Blood throbbed in his head as the rope carried on rattling upwards. Far below, he saw Billie hurry towards the wings and plunge an arm offstage.

'The men who tied Harry meant no harm to him!' she cried out to the audience. 'They tied him as we instructed, that was all. But we are his friends, and we'll make things more exciting—what else are friends for?'

She pulled out a bow and arrow. It was from another of the theatre's acts, a Native American dance scene, but the arrow was dipped in pitch, and flaming. Billie let the arrow fly straight at the rope just above Harry's tied ankles, and it glanced against it. Doused in oil, the rope caught light, smoke curling up into the fly tower, as the arrow arched down into a bucket of water held by Arthur. Harry heard shouts from the audience, and he saw one of the men who had tied him standing in the aisle, waving his arms in dismay. *Time to get started.*

Harry unclenched his muscles and let out the breath he had kept inside him ever since the first rope had been tied. For as long as the men had been working on him, he had kept every muscle locked tight, and his ribcage had been expanded to its maximum size too, filled with as much breath as he could muster. But his muscles softened now, and his ribs and stomach sank inwards, releasing vital space. The knots were still rigid, but the ropes no longer gripped so hard, and the very corner of his elbow had already slid free.

'More excitement! Provided by his loyal friends!' cried Arthur, as he and Billie dragged a large saw, nearly twelve feet long, out from the wings on the other side of the stage. Each end was wedged in a heavy block of wood, so that its razor-sharp teeth were upright, and Harry's friends positioned it directly beneath him. *Found backstage, being used to cut wood for some Arabian palace scenery*, thought Harry, with a faint upside-down smile. The audience was bellowing now, and the man was stumbling down the aisle towards the stage, some of the others who had done the tying running after him. But Harry looked up at the rope above his feet, burning quickly now, and he knew they would never make it in time.

His elbow was free, allowing a hand to swivel downwards. He gripped the nearest knot, one of the American ones he knew well, and his fingers dug between the loops and twists, quickly finding the weakest spot. Harry pulled hard and a loop loosened. Immediately his fingers were performing the knot backwards, an exact reverse of those loops and twists until the rope came away. His arm was now free, and his other arm could move, too. No time to do all the knots, or even a quarter of them, but the trick was to spot the ones that would slacken the ropes by the maximum amount if untied. His eyes darted about, searching for which one that might be. The one by his hip, he decided—unfortunately it was one of the unfamiliar English ones.

He snapped his eyes shut. He pictured the pattern of the knot as clearly as he could. His eyes opened again, and his fingers went to work, delving into the knot. It was harder than he expected and he wondered if he had remembered wrongly. Harry's fingers dug deeper and he grimaced as one of his nails bent backwards, about to snap—

But it didn't, not quite. It held, and a loop of knot pulled free. The other ropes loosened too and now his upper body wriggled free. His lower half was still tied— *no need to worry about that*. Still upside-down, Harry threw his upper body upwards with all his strength, and his hands grabbed the hook by his ankles, as the rope above burned down to its last threads. He pulled, and his ankles lifted free, his body swinging down after them, the right way up at last. He kicked out his tied legs, making the rope swing and, when he had swung out far enough, let go.

He plummeted downwards, landing on a feather mattress which had been dragged out of the wings by Billie and Arthur, just in time. Harry sat up, heard a clang and saw the hook had fallen too, hitting the saw. A short length of burning rope trailed from it. Billie and Arthur pulled Harry to his feet and the crowd roared. Together, a little unsteadily because of the bouncy mattress, they performed their usual bow.

The bottom of the curtain thumped down onto the stage. Stagehands were lifting away the saw, a dancer dressed as a Native American retrieved her bow and arrow and the next act was hurrying onto the stage, a lady with a performing poodle. Harry pulled off the rest of the ropes and marched into the wings with his friends. He walked along a corridor, climbed several flights of a rickety staircase, and then pushed through a door into their dressing room, right up at the top of the Trilby Theatre, Constant Lane. It was a little dark and cold, and the furniture was worn, but the room was comfortable enough, and the theatre management had left logs, paper and kindling by the fireplace. Harry knelt down and started building a fire, carefully arranging the pieces of kindling in the grate, with fingers still red and sore from unpicking the ropes.

'Definitely not a bad place to stay,' he said. 'Told you it was worth keeping those press reviews, Artie.'

'Yes, and we might get some from the London papers now.' Arthur waved a folder, stuffed with clippings from the New York and New Orleans press. 'I reckon we could get a performing slot at any theatre in Europe.'

'No wonder the management threw in a meal,' said Billie, crossing to a trolley in the corner, grabbing a piece of bread, and lifting the lid off the soup tureen. Plumes of steam wafted out. 'Hm, pumpkin soup.'

'Tasty. And this is a pretty comfy chair too, if you don't mind a bit of dust.' Arthur lowered himself into an armchair and the cushions released wafts of dust and mould. 'We could get pretty cosy, hanging around here. Not that we'll get the chance for that—once we get started, I mean.'

The dusty clouds lingered around him. Through them, Harry saw crinkles of concentration gather on his friend's forehead as Arthur pulled out his note-book, and flicked through his notes. Nearby, Billie seemed more relaxed at first, dropping into another chair with the bread in her hand; but she wasn't eating it, just resting it against her lips. They had been like this ever since the press conference, Harry reflected; even in the wings, waiting to perform, they had been thoughtful, preoccupied. Smiling, he carried on con-structing the fire.

'You're right, Harry, it's pretty odd,' Billie said. 'Mr James saying all that stuff on the train, about us having troubled pasts and so on. I thought it was strange at the time—'

'And then a few hours later we bump into the Benevolent Orphans,' Arthur butted in. 'Who turn out to be a society *full* of people with troubled pasts, and who are determined to help other folk out in the noblest of ways.'

'But why's Mr James making such a big deal of it? Saying it's the perfect case for us, or whatever it was.' Billie tossed her bread in the air and caught it. 'We'd investigate anyway.'

'He might be trying to spur us on.' Harry crumpled some paper into a ball, and pushed it between the kindling. 'Maybe he needs us to work even harder on this case.'

'Work harder?' Billie frowned. 'We worked pretty hard on the last one, back in New Orleans. We risked everything to sort that out, and a good thing too.'

'Yes, but Billie, maybe the Order reckons this investigation is even more important,' Arthur said. 'I've been reading more about this Benevolent Orphans society in the newspapers—it really is an incredible organization. People have written in, saying how much they've been helped by them, by their hospitals, libraries, campaigns for world peace. It must be about the most worthy organization there is, I reckon.'

'You're right, it's not only a few kindly old folk we're trying to help.' Billie sat back in her chair. 'It's anyone who might one day benefit from the work they do—and that's a lot of people.'

'Absolutely.' Arthur leant back in his chair, steepling his fingers. 'It's quite a responsibility.'

Harry positioned the last piece of kindling.

Distracted by his friends' conversation, he had built the pile a bit taller than it needed to be, and it was slightly lopsided too, but it would flicker to life quickly enough, once he set light to it. He glanced round at the others, who were still lost in their thoughts, Arthur's steepled fingers resting against the deepest crinkle in his forehead, Billie still rotating that piece of bread in her hand. With another smile, he looked around the room.

'Anyone seen the matches?' he asked.

Arthur spotted a box of them on a shelf near his chair and threw them to Harry. He picked the box up, took out a match, and placed its end against the box's side. But he didn't strike it.

His eyes narrowed, peering into the fireplace. Rattling sounds echoed out of the chimney, and soot scattered over his lopsided tower. Still on his knees, Harry shuffled back. There were a few more rattles and clunks, followed by a furious fizzling sound. Harry toppled back onto the floor as something smashed onto his tower, sending the kindling flying.

It was smooth, oval-shaped, metal, the size of a fist. A thick stub of cord trailed from it, its end blazing with sparks and flame so powerfully that a bit of kindling caught light. On the object's surface was a circle of letters. The first one was an 'M', and Harry had no difficulty reading the rest of them now. '*Magwell*,' he read.

'That . . . ' Arthur stuttered, 'is a BOMB!'

Chapter Six

'That cord—it's a fuse!' Arthur cried.

Harry leapt forward and tried to snuff out the flaming cord with his finger and thumb, but it was blazing too fiercely and he pulled his hand away with a shout. He grabbed a cushion from a nearby chair and stuffed that onto the fuse instead, but the cushion caught fire.

'You've got to put it out!' Artie shouted.

'How can I? It's too powerful!' Harry threw the flaming cushion into the grate.

'So let's run!' Billie said.

'Too late! We won't be able to get far enough!' cried Arthur.

'Th-throw the bomb out the window then—' Billie stuttered.

'NO.' Harry stumbled to his feet. 'It'll explode near whoever's out there, won't it?'

'Take it apart, Artie!' Billie cried. 'Maybe you can disconnect the fuse or—'

'Impossible, I'd need special tools!' Arthur was pinning himself to the wall. 'And there's no time anyway—it's nearly burnt its way into the bomb!'

Harry's arms shot forward, picking up the metal oval. Angling it, he saw that Arthur was right; the blazing stub had burnt down almost to the point where it would enter inside. Too thick to cut, impossible to put out . . . .

Or maybe not.

'Billie! The pumpkin soup!' he shouted.

Harry dropped the bomb and kicked it up with his left boot. The bomb arced across the room. His eyes flicked ahead of it, to see if Billie had understood the words he had yelled out.

Of course she had.

Billie was snatching the lid off the soup tureen. Harry hadn't had time to aim his kick properly and the bomb was a good inch off-target, but that was what Billie was for. She held up the lid at exactly the right angle, and the bomb clanged off it, dropped into the tureen, and disappeared into the orange soup with a plop.

Harry didn't move, his left boot in the air, his hand still burning, the skin where he had touched the fuse puffy and white. Arthur was still flat against the wall; Billie held the tureen's lid. All of them waited.

Nothing happened. Billie dropped the lid with another clang, picked a ladle off the trolley, and fished the bomb out.

'That's all right then.' She held it up, dripping. 'Not sure I fancy the soup anymore though—'

Harry hurled up the nearest window sash, swung through, and climbed the drainpipe running up the building's side. Billie and Arthur called after him but the sounds faded as he clambered higher. Soon, all he could hear was his own breathing, the scrambling of his boots against metal, and the grind of the pipe's brackets against the brickwork. He jumped onto the roof. It was slanted and his boots slithered on the tiles as he stumbled towards the nearby chimney stacks, trying to work out which one might lead down to their dressing room. Harry spotted one a few yards away, almost exactly above where the dressing room would be. He reached it and spun round, searching for the slightest movement, but there was nothing. How long had it been since someone had been standing at this chimney, dropping the lethal item down it? A minute at most, he calculated.

And a minute's a long time, if you're quick.

Harry saw him. A caped figure standing on another

roof entirely, several buildings away. The night sky was heavy with cloud, smothering the moon, but a few rays shone through, picking out the shape. It was the same person Harry had seen outside the St Pancras Hotel a few hours earlier, he was sure of it. The man was at least six feet tall, with arms crossed commandingly, legs planted apart, the cape rippling in the breeze, its corner turning back to reveal a red lining. The face was in shadow, but one side of it bulged in the same misshapen way, and this time Harry saw why. A cloth mask covered the lower half of the man's face, but it was slanted so that it rose diagonally right up to the top of one side of his head, swelling with something underneath—

Harry's boots lost their grip. He slithered downwards, scrabbling at the tiles before regaining his grip. When he looked back, the figure had gone.

Chapter Seven

The cab clattered up to the kerb, the horses' hooves striking the cobbles. Harry waited by the stage door of the theatre, checking the street's doorways, its windows, and the alleyways leading off it. Beside him, Billie edged forward, but Harry put out a hand and held her back.

'Wait,' he said. 'The theatre folk—they want to check.'

A light rain fell, and the alleyways and windows were particularly dark. Men from the theatre had hurried out with umbrellas, some talking worriedly to the cab driver, others inspecting the cab itself and checking underneath for signs of anything suspicious. Their hands shook, Harry noticed—just hearing about what had happened to their fellow performers the previous night had horrified them, and they were keen to help in any way they could. As the inspection continued,

Harry leant out further, glanced up the street, and pulled back again.

'Ground squirrels, that's what we are.' Billie managed a smile. 'Saw them out on the Arkansas prairie, spending all day peering out of their holes, checking this way and that, making sure it was safe.'

'What were they frightened of?'

'Coyotes. Swooping birds of prey. Can't blame them for being careful, really. Can't blame you and me either, when you remember what's after us—'

Harry flashed forward, pulling Billie with him. The theatre folk had nodded, and in a few steps he and Billie were inside the cab. A brief knock against its wooden insides sent it rattling off down the street, while Harry ran his fingers over the cushioned seats, even though the theatre folk had checked them already. He sat so that he could keep watching the street as it moved past the window, but without too much of him being visible from outside. Billie was trying to do the same, but wobbling a bit.

'At least ground squirrels know what they're looking out for,' she said, peering about. 'No mistaking a coyote or some big bird. Harder for us. A cape, a mask—apart from that we know pretty much nothing, I'd say.'

'That'll change.' Harry checked his watch.

'Arthur'll have discovered something—he's been working for nearly three hours now.'

'Let's hope so.' Billie flumped back on the seat, and cracked her knuckles with frustration. 'Can hardly do worse than you and me.'

'I know, I was there,' said Harry. Slow, detailed, methodical work wasn't his strongest skill, and that was even more true of Billie, and so the morning they had just spent searching the roof for clues had been a difficult one. They had started at dawn, as soon as there was light enough to see. Every roof tile had been checked, every bit of brickwork had been studied, and the task had been made even slower by the fact that only one of them could search at a time, the other needing to watch the surrounding roofs and windows, ground-squirrel-like, knowing they would be easy targets in such an exposed spot, and the assassin could easily return. Tense and nervous, they had searched on, and Harry had even climbed halfway down into the chimney that led to the dressing room to see whether there was any evidence lodged in its crevices. There wasn't and so, after three hours' searching, they still knew nothing about their attacker.

But he knows about us, Harry thought, as the cab lurched round a corner, and he carried on peering out of the window. He remembered that moment on a

different rooftop the previous day—the rooftop opposite 24 Rigby Gardens, where he had spotted the bullet
casings. Had that caped figure been hidden somewhere, watching him as he crept forward from the
chimney stack, trying to see those gleaming shapes?
And then there had been that moment at the press
conference, when he had leapt to his feet and called
out that question, drawing attention to himself and
his friends. The man could have followed them to the
theatre, watched their act and observed their skills—a
little research might even have somehow uncovered
their connection to the Order of the White Crow. The
cab clattered on, and all these possibilities circled in
Harry's thoughts, some likely, some less so.

*But one thing's certain. Whoever's after the Benevolent
Orphans came after us, too.*

'We're here, Harry,' Billie said, a few moments
later, as the carriage rattled to a halt.

University College. Harry saw another grey London
building with wide stone steps, a row of pillars across
the front, and a lofty dome. Men in gowns and mortar
boards hurried through its gates. Opening the cab's
door, Harry checked in every direction before handing the driver his fare, and then darted through the
gates and up the college building steps. A few minutes
later, he and Billie were crossing a marble lobby

towards a pair of bronze doors, over which the arched word *Laboratories* was written. Next to those doors, some porters worked behind a desk, and they looked up at Harry and Billie in a not particularly friendly way. Harry marched right up to them.

'We're here to see Arthur Dale-Roberts.'

'Ah—Master Arthur's friends? Come this way!'

The suspicious looks vanished. Papers were shuffled, visitors' badges were pinned to Harry's and Billie's clothes, and one of the porters led them through the doors and into the college's corridors. Doors flashed past, ajar, and Harry glimpsed equipment-crammed laboratories with more gowned men bent over fizzing glass vessels.

'This way—if you are here to help Mister Arthur, we must not delay. His work will be of great interest; it always is!'

Harry exchanged a quick smile with Billie. It hadn't been easy for Arthur, growing up as he had, tugged around different cities by his father; but the one advantage was that the studious boy had become familiar with some of the most important places of learning and research in the world, building up an extraordinary range of knowledge in his neat, careful mind, along with the skill to seek out even more knowledge by using the resources of corridors and rooms like these. The porter was heading towards a door at a passage's end, and Harry saw its frosted glass flicker with a greenish light. Curious fizzing noises could be heard. The porter ushered them inside. Arthur was sitting at a laboratory bench, wearing a pair of darkened goggles, reading a book with one hand and carrying out an experiment with the other, holding a lit Bunsen burner under a glass vessel containing something that bubbled and fumed. Nearby on the bench Harry saw the dismantled bits and pieces of the bomb, each carefully labelled.

'Sorry about the fumes, Plumridge.' Arthur pushed the goggles up his forehead and peered at the porter.

'It's quite all right Master Arthur—all part of the noble business of scientific enquiry.' The porter bowed. 'May I enquire what your current research concerns? My colleagues and I are always keen to know.'

'Oh nothing serious—just investigating a particularly brutal and ingenious attempted murder.' Arthur laughed in an over-the-top way, and threw a cloth over the bits of bomb. 'Ho ho ho.'

'Ho ho ho indeed, sir,' chuckled the porter as he shuffled out of the room, closing the door behind him. The smile immediately vanished from Arthur's face, and he pulled his goggles down again.

'We've had a very lucky escape,' he said.

He tugged the cloth away, revealing the bits of bomb again. Its metal outside lay in two halves next to various other components, pieces of wire and metal tubes. Next to them, a green powder sat in a small corked glass vessel, which Arthur tapped with an extremely tiny spoon.

'It's not actually a bomb—a grenade is the correct term. Anyway, I've isolated the explosive charge; it's this green stuff and it's pretty powerful. Harmless unless a naked flame touches it, but if that happens—' He uncorked the tube, dipped in the spoon, and fished out the tiniest amount of the powder, a couple of grains. 'So this is what that fuse was burning its way towards, before the pumpkin soup snuffed it out. Have a look.'

He moved the spoon across to a small iron box with a thick sheet of plate glass at the front and various dials and gauges on top. Opening a flap at one side, Arthur inserted the spoon. Through the plate glass, Harry saw the tiny granules tip onto a little wire mesh, suspended in the box. Arthur sealed the flap and handed Harry and Billie their own goggles, which they slid on as Arthur flicked a switch on the box's side. A flame flickered under the wire mesh. The granules glowed, and then the box flashed, shuddered violently, and went dark with smoke. The various dials on its top all swung to their maximum settings.

'That's just two grains of it,' said Arthur. 'Inside the grenade, there was almost four hundred times that amount. Enough to blow up our dressing room, and all the rooms around it, as well.'

'He sure did want to get rid of us,' Billie said, pushing up her goggles.

'Us and everything about us.' Arthur pushed his up too, and his expression was grim. He tapped his jacket where his notebook was kept. 'Any notes I might have taken, for example—gone. Plus the grenade itself, of course—didn't want to leave any evidence of it, did he? But *that* didn't work out for him.'

He reached along the bench for one of the sections of the metal orb. Carefully, his fingers rotated it, revealing the circle of engraved letters Harry had noticed as the grenade tumbled into the grate with its blazing fuse—the same circle of letters he had half-deciphered on the base of the bullet casings. They were perfectly clear now, and they grew even clearer as Arthur hovered a magnifying glass over them, making them bulge.

Magwell.

'Wish I'd made it out earlier. On the bullet casings, I mean,' said Harry.

'Don't worry, we've seen it now,' said Arthur. 'We know that the same name's on the bullets, and that's an important piece of information. Particularly when you discover who or what this Magwell is. Come on, over here.'

He tugged off his goggles and walked down to the other end of the bench, to a large pile of books. Harry followed him. Important though the grenade was, it only told them what they already knew: that this assassin was extremely dangerous. But now Arthur was turning his attention to something very different, an actual clue—the only one they had been able to find, despite all the searching he and Billie had done. Joining Arthur, Harry saw that he had marked the pages in several books with yellow slips of paper. Arthur tugged across the first of these marked books, and opened it up.

'These are government records of all the licensed makers of weapons and explosives in Europe. Arms manufacturers, in other words. The college keeps them as part of its library on industrial processes, and everything's listed here: the devices, the factories they're made in, the lot. There's other information too, details of any insignia or symbols, for example. And the symbol we're looking for is right here, look.'

His finger tapped it. The same name, the same letters, arranged in the same circle; it was printed neatly in the book. *Magwell.* Underneath it, a column of information was printed, and Arthur's finger stopped tapping and swept downwards as he told them the key facts.

'Magwell's Machines, that's the company's name. An arms business set up by Ernest Magwell, one of the world's most successful makers of deadly weapons. Rifles, bombs, pistols, and even weapons no one's heard of yet—a silently firing rifle, maybe, or a high-powered grenade? Anyway, Magwell's men invent them, his factories build them, and he sells them all over the world to governments of countries making war, or to anyone who'll buy them—he's a rich man. Tests all his weapons himself apparently—one of them even went wrong back at the start of his career, wounding him.' Arthur lifted his finger, which was blackened with ink. 'And once he's tested the weapons to his satisfaction, he mass-produces them and sells them. The weapons from his factory go on to be responsible for the deaths of thousands of people.'

'That's horrible,' Billie said. 'But does it actually help us? All it tells us is that whoever is launching these attacks on the Benevolent Orphans, and us, bought his weapons from Magwell's firm. Like all sorts of horrible people do around the world—it could be anyone.'

'But that's why the grenade is so interesting.' Arthur tapped the page. 'It's an extremely sophisticated piece of machinery; I've never seen anything like it. And there's no mention of it in these records. It's a secret weapon, in other words, something he's only recently invented. And that's probably true of the rifle used to kill Dame Flora without a sound being heard—like I've said, people have been trying to invent a rifle that fires silently for years and if Magwell's cracked it, then that's another secret weapon. These aren't any old weapons from Magwell's Machines, in other words—they're the company's very latest inventions, probably a handful in existence.'

'So this Magwell will have a fairly good idea who's got hold of these weapons.' Harry nodded. 'Makes sense that if he's only made a few, then he'll know who bought them.'

'That's right—not that he's going to tell us.' Arthur walked back to the grenade components. 'And obviously, just because he might know who he sold them to, that won't help us if those people then sold them to someone else, and then that person sold them to someone *else*—I didn't say I'd worked it all out. But it's worth investigating more. Particularly as Magwell's latest factory has just opened right here in London six months ago—wait, I need to store this stuff safely; I want to keep it for further investigation.'

He was tipping the green powder in the glass vessel

into a metal tube, about five inches long. Once it was in, he started screwing tight the tube's lid. While he did this, Harry picked up the next book on the pile, *Journal of London Factories 1885*. He opened it at the marked place and found a photographic plate, showing a small gathering of wealthy-looking gentlemen on the steps of a factory. *Investors gather at the first day of construction at Magwell's Machines, London,* the caption said. Harry studied it while Billie peered over his shoulder.

'Is that him?' Harry pointed at a figure right at the centre of the photograph. 'Magwell, I mean?'

'That's him.' Arthur glanced across briefly as he slid the metal tube carefully into his pocket. 'The man in charge of one of Europe's biggest arms businesses, who may or may not know something about what we're investigating—what are you thinking, Harry?'

Harry said nothing. But his finger remained where it was, next to the figure in the photograph. He was a tall man of about fifty years, and in some ways his face was an unremarkable one: a slender nose, a small moustache directly beneath it. But in other ways, it was very unusual indeed. *Tests all his weapons himself . . . One of them went wrong . . . wounding him . . .* Harry went back for Arthur's magnifying glass, and held it over the grainy image of the man's face, particularly the left side.

It was covered with a huge scar. Thick tissue slanted all the way up from his chin to the top of his left ear, a disturbing, unsettling sight. A diagonal scar that would be noticed by anyone who saw that face, and would have to be covered by something diagonal . . .

A mask? A slanted one? Harry bent closer over the book, holding the magnifying glass nearer, trying to make out more detail, but the image just blurred.

'Well, Harry? What are you thinking?'

Harry said nothing. It was a hunch, that was all, and a hunch based on the briefest glimpse of the assassin, in feeble moonlight. He could so easily have been mistaken, so he decided not to mention it to his friends for now, in case they became distracted by it, and perhaps missed some other, more definite piece of information.

'So where is this factory?' he said, closing the book.

'I thought you might ask that. Hoxton, about two miles from here,' Arthur replied. 'I can pretty much guess what you're planning—'

'I can too,' said Billie, with a smile.

'All right then.' Arthur nervously checked his watch. 'But, given that it's a factory manufacturing some of the most dangerous weapons in the known world, I really do think we should wait until after dark.'

Chapter Eight

Harry stepped down from the cab. Gas lamps flickered along the street, but the nearby buildings were inkily black, only the occasional glimmer in their windows. His muscles twitched after being cooped up, and after all the waiting around in the university laboratories. Billie stepped down beside him, also looking restless. Arthur, closing the door of the cab, held them both back.

'Wait until he's out of sight, just in case,' he muttered, as the driver cracked his whip and the cab rattled off.

'But the factory's several streets away—we deliberately didn't get him to drop us right there,' whispered Billie.

'What if he heard us talking about that? Some listening device inside the cab, perhaps. We're up against an assassin who can use modern weaponry.' Arthur fingered the grenade components inside his jacket. 'He can easily recruit local cab drivers as spies.'

Harry watched the cab disappear round the corner. The rattling of its wheels faded into the sounds of the night: barking dogs, hissing gas lamps, the muttering of voices behind the glimmering windows. Harry and his friends set off along the street, Arthur taking out a folded sheet of paper and opening it up. It was an architectural drawing, found in the college library's section on City Planning.

'It used to be a perfectly ordinary factory until Magwell bought it,' he said. 'It says in small writing, down in the corner here. A steelworks—it made spoons, knives, and forks, that sort of thing.'

'Plenty of windows, and they look easy to reach.' Billie peered at the plan with an expert eye. 'Ooh, a break-in, and at night! Reminds me of the Kansas City Hat Shop Shakedown—have I told you that one?'

'A few times,' said Harry, scanning the shadows. But Billie's stories could be useful at times like these; they helped stop them from getting nervous, especially Artie.

'Nothing to do with stealing—I was getting what I was owed,' Billie launched in. 'Worked all afternoon in the back of that shop, dipping nearly four hundred yards of lace in dye, stirring it in a stinking barrel. Had to keep popping out for fresh air because of the fumes, so I couldn't get it finished by the end of the day, and then the owner said he wasn't paying me for any of it, not a cent! Drinking fellow he was, always swigging out of a bottle, and I know about drinking fellows, so I waited for him to go up to his office at sundown, and waited some more, an hour or so. Then I scrambled up a drainpipe through a window and there he was, snoring in his chair, empty bottle on his desk, another dangling from his hand. Helped myself to the cash box, took what I was owed, not a cent extra, although I did dress him up in one of those frilly bonnets his factory made, and left him like that for his staff to find in the morning— finishing touches like that matter, don't you think?'

'They do,' said Harry. 'But I'm not sure we're going to have time for that sort of thing tonight. This is no hat shop we're breaking into.'

'That's right,' agreed Arthur. 'And here it is.'

They were peering out of an alleyway. A drab building towered across the street, several storeys high. At its far end, some workers were leaving through the main door and hurrying into the gas-lit gloom. A few of the factory's windows were lit, but the rest were dark. Arthur checked the architectural drawing.

'The factory floor, where they actually build the stuff, should be down *there*.' He indicated the front of the building. 'We want the offices, which are where the paperwork will be.' His finger moved across to the drawing's other end, where he had drawn a cross. 'All about sales and the customers who buy the weapons and . . . '

'Wait here, Artie,' said Billie. 'Might take us a while to get things ready, and we don't want you getting jumpy, hanging about in the open. We'll call you when we're done.'

She headed across the street, Harry just behind her. Together, they kept their pace steady, so that no one glimpsing them might suspect they were doing anything but wandering by. But Harry's eyes were darting all over the building, checking for the easiest way into the section Arthur had pointed out. He chose a row of windows near a drainpipe, and hurried across.

Harry held out a hand. Billie delved in her pocket and fished out a piece of string with a copper ring tied in the end, extracted from a piece of laboratory equipment back at the college. She dropped this device into his hand, and they started climbing the drainpipe— Harry in front, Billie close behind. A few minutes later they were level with the first window and jumped onto the sill. Billie ran her fingers along the top of the window sash, checking for any gaps between it and the surrounding frame.

'Too tight,' she said. 'Next one looks better.'

They leapt onto the next sill. Just as Billie had said, there was a narrow gap at the top of this one; Harry lifted up the string, and pushed the copper ring through. It was a tight fit and it took a bit of wiggling, which wasn't easy with the two of them balanced on the narrow sill. But after a few seconds, the ring was through and Harry saw it dangling a few inches from his nose, on the other side of the glass. Billie fed the string through her fingers and the ring lowered down, swaying and tapping against the pane.

It arrived by the latch at the bottom. Billie narrowed her eyes, twiddling the string between finger and thumb so that it rotated, and the ring at the string's other end rotated too. On the other side of the glass, it bumped against the metal latch, bounced off, then caught hold. Harry and Billie tugged the string hard, and the ring pulled the latch free. Harry slid the window up, and then waited for Billie, who was waving down to Arthur in the street. Three minutes later, their friend had clambered to the top of the dra inpipe, a little out of breath, and Billie was guiding him onto the first sill, and then to the second. Harry helped Arthur through the open window into the corridor inside. Arthur slithered, and Harry heard a floorboard creak as his friend landed. He was about to follow him, when he heard Billie hissing in his ear.

'Look, Harry!'

She was pointing towards the factory's main gate, which was locked now. Harry narrowed his eyes and saw a familiar figure, moving up to it with a distinctive heavy walk.

'That policeman! Newton!' Billie said.

It was him, unquestionably. The street was dark, but there was a gas lamp next to the gate, and its flickers picked out those steel buttons and that intricate shoulder braid. Harry made out the police inspector's burly shape and mutton-chop beard. They watched as Newton walked right up to the gate and pulled on a piece of cord. Somewhere in the dark building, a bell jangled.

'What's he doing here?' Billie hissed.

'Investigating the Rigby Gardens murder, same as us,' Harry murmured. His eyes had focused directly on Inspector Newton's left hand, which was down by his jacket pocket. *The pocket where he slid those bullet casings.*

'Hardly the same as us. He's a policeman demanding to be let in, and we're three kids breaking in like thieves.' Billie pressed herself close to the brickwork. 'I don't think he'd be too happy to know we were here, do you?'

'He *is* the same as us,' Harry said. 'He's following clues—pretty much the same clues, too. We found the letters on the grenade, he found them on those bullet casings, and that's why we've all ended up here, at this factory. Although you're right, Billie—he's able to do it officially.'

'Maybe.' Billie narrowed her eyes. 'But it's pretty late to make an official visit—everyone's gone home. We're breaking in, so we obviously had to wait until dark, but why's *he* waited until now? Why didn't he call round during the day?'

Harry nodded. There were other odd things about Newton: the way he was ringing the bell over and over and then stepping away from it, the way he kept glancing up and down the street. Harry saw that he was deliberately stepping into the darkest possible spot, away from the gas lamp's feeble glow, before marching back up to the bell cord again.

But then Newton's wait was over. The gate rattled, and slid open. Newton hurried in.

Time for the unofficial investigation to start, too, Harry thought. He turned back to the window and, together with Billie, stepped inside.

Chapter Nine

'That was pretty quick work.' Billie dropped down into the dark corridor. 'Might make a good story one day, you never know.'

'Shouldn't be too hard to play up—dodging a police chief, breaking into an arms factory, investigating a murder,' said Harry, landing beside her. 'I'll leave the window up, in case we have to get out in a hurry—'

He grabbed Billie's arm. She had stepped forward, and a floorboard had creaked under her feet. The same creaking noise that Arthur had made when he slid inside a few minutes earlier; it drifted into the factory's darkness. Harry and Billie waited, listening, but there was no sound of anyone coming. Harry double-checked the window sash, making sure it was open high enough for them to slide out easily if they were disturbed. Then he and Billie made their way up the corridor.

'Looks like Artie's made a good start,' Billie whispered.

Along the corridor, a door was open and Arthur could be seen, hurrying about inside. *Records,* a sign on the door said, and Harry pushed through it to find a room crowded with filing cabinets, some reaching all the way to the ceiling. Arthur was carefully sliding the drawers open, tugging various papers out, examining their contents, riffling through.

'It might take some time to find out what we need,' he said. 'All I've done so far is familiarize myself with their cataloguing system; it's tricky working out how arms manufacturers organize their information. Designs for weapons seem to be over on this side of the room.' He pulled out another drawer. 'There's a whole stack of information here, but at least it's almost all in English. As for the rest, that's in French, Italian, or German so I should be able to get through that pretty quickly, too. Ah, look—these are recent contracts, all lined up by date. Maybe a recent contract will be for a recently invented weapon—that's a reasonable expectation?'

Harry and Billie exchanged smiles in the gloom. Their friend was hard at work, his hands scampering through the files, and Harry couldn't help thinking that, in their own way, those fingers were every bit as nimble as his own, performing some trick. Opening a drawer himself, he flicked open a file, and his smile faded. Inside were various technical drawings of objects that he could see were weapons, pistols of various designs. The bullets for the guns were detailed too, tidily drawn in draughtsman's ink. Harry looked around at the other nearby cabinets, the other drawers. *Each containing many more neatly drawn designs of weapons to be distributed all over the world, drawings responsible for the deaths of thousands of people . . .*

'Hm, this is taking longer than I hoped. But this might be the rifle, I think.'

Arthur was holding a file, and had lifted a paper from it. On it, another neat drawing, this one of a long, thin rifle with a curious barrel shape around its muzzle. Arthur was studying it, intrigued.

'Yes, here we are. A silent rifle—it looks like Magwell really has cracked it. All to do with the way the bulky barrel muffles vibrations, I guess. Clever—although also completely horrible.' Arthur straightened, and held the design away. 'This must be the weapon that killed poor Dame Flora while she watered her chrysanthemums— were those the bullet casings you saw, Harry?'

He pointed at the side of the design, and Harry saw neat sketches of the casings, the exact size and shape as the ones he had seen on the roof.

'That's them—but who's bought it, this rifle?' Harry asked.

'It doesn't say. Not in this file, anyway.' Arthur tucked the paper under his arm and headed off across the room. 'Sales are in a completely different section, all the way over here. I'll have to sort through them— maybe this rifle has a serial number, and I can find out who's bought it that way. But it's not going to be quick . . . .'

He hesitated in front of a new set of filing cabinets, checking the labels on their fronts. He started easing the drawers open again, and riffling through. For some time, the only noise that could be heard was the soft rustling of papers against fingertips. Billie, bored, paced around the room for a bit, and then sank onto a chair. She found some pencils, and built a tower out of them. Harry went back to the door and waited there, watching and listening in case anyone came. He mused over what he and his friends had discovered so far, moving the different pieces of information about in his mind. *Newton. That pale hand. A caped man. A grenade rattling down a chimney . . .*

'Well I never,' Arthur said.

Harry swung round, unsure how long he had been lost in thought. He saw that Arthur had moved down almost five cabinets from where he had been previously, and that he was holding another file in his hand, papers slithering out of it, a few of them scattering onto the floor. Arthur's eyes were fixed on the papers that remained in his grip.

'What is it?' Billie was next to him, studying the papers. 'A list of people who've bought the rifle?'

'Nothing to do with the rifle at all—haven't found that stuff yet. But I came across this. It could be nothing. Probably just a coincidence.' Arthur pulled another paper from the file, and squinted at it.

'Tell us anyway.' Harry left the door to join the others.

'Well, it's one of these recent contracts. I couldn't help noticing it, as I was flicking through.' Arthur tapped the grey file. 'It's very recent in fact, as far as I can see—negotiated just a month ago. And it's big. Nearly seven thousand weapons, and big quantities of ammunition.'

'Seven thousand weapons?' Billie frowned. 'But we're after someone who bought just one or two weapons, Artie, and not ordinary ones—special newly invented ones. Don't get distracted.'

'I'm not getting distracted.' Arthur pulled another paper out of the file, and his eyes widened. 'Actually, this could be really important. It could mean we'd be wise to get out of here, apart from anything else.'

'What are you saying, Artie?' Harry asked. He tried to read some of the papers but they were incomprehensible, even the alphabet unrecognizable. 'Tell us what you're thinking—this big contract, who's it for?'

'Who's it for? That's why it's taking so long to tell you anything useful about it—the papers are mainly in Russian, and that's by far my least favourite language,' said Arthur, squinting harder at the papers. 'But it's also why it's so important. Because Russian's the language they speak in Ravelstan, you see—and this contract's with the king of Ravelstan's army, for their war to stop the people of West Ravelstan breaking free.'

Ravelstan. Arthur had whispered the word in the gloomy office. But Harry heard it echoing off the marble walls of another place entirely, the conference room of the Hotel St Pancras. *The tragic country of Ravelstan, so terribly afflicted by war* . . . He heard the cry of Lord Jaspar, leader of the Benevolent Orphans, and he remembered Arthur's quick explanation of the brutal conflict, and he recalled the other key piece of information about Ravelstan too, the one that Arthur was plainly thinking about now.

'Dame Flora—she was working there,' Harry said. 'She'd set up one of her hospitals and she was helping people, saving them from that war—'

'That extremely horrible war. There's a map

showing one of the battlefields right here.' Arthur drew out another document, and shuddered. 'The king of Ravelstan's ministers have folded it into the contract, to provide information on how the weapons need to be used.'

'It doesn't necessarily tell us anything.' Billie frowned at the map, labelled in Russian. 'So Dame Flora was setting up a hospital in Ravelstan, to help people wounded in the war. That doesn't mean she was involved with the politics and money *behind* the war. As for Magwell being the one who was supplying the weapons—that could be coincidence, like Artie said.'

'It could be . . . ' Arthur had found another paper, and was reading it. His face had gone pale. 'But have a look at this.'

He handed Harry and Billie the paper. It was a letter, written in English, with a spidery, jabbing hand.

To Mr Ernest Magwell, Esq.,
For some weeks now, you have refused my attempts to meet with you. You will regret this profoundly. My passion for the freedom-seeking people of West Ravelstan has never been more powerfully felt. Governments around the world have condemned the king of Ravelstan's war against them, and supplying him with weapons is now

banned—and yet I have proof that you exploit your powerful connections to secretly do just that. Here in London, those in power turn a blind eye to your factory's doings—well, not I. Let it be known that I shall stop at nothing to expose your company's wicked tradings, forcing those in power to bring you to heel—and I have the goodly might of the Benevolent Orphans behind me, all of whom will support my cause. End your illegal involvement with this war, or the suffering that your weapons cause will be given voice; this you shall witness.

Yours faithfully,

Dame Flora Cusp

Harry finished the letter. He immediately went back and read it again, and he saw from Billie's darting eyes that she was doing the same. For some time, no one said anything. Then Arthur, trying not to get nervous, attempted a shrug.

'Obviously, it could still be a coincidence. It doesn't actually prove anything—'

'Of course it proves something!' Billie spluttered. 'You were there at the press conference, Artie! You heard how much Dame Flora cared about the war in Ravelstan! Now we know she was trying to stop Magwell selling weapons to it and—'

'Remember Lord Jaspar, and his campaign for world peace,' said Harry. 'He said he was working with Dame Flora to stop the Ravelstan war. That was the whole point of the conference he was setting up in Paris. Maybe he was behind the ban on supplying arms—how big is that contract with the king of Ravelstan's army again?'

'Big, very big, and valuable.' Arthur was looking nervous. 'I know it looks bad. But just because Magwell had a reason to carry out the crime, it doesn't necessarily mean that he did. There's no actual evidence, that's what I'm saying—'

'Oh yes there is,' said Billie. 'How about the fact that Dame Flora ended up dead, shot by a rifle made by Magwell's own company? That's evidence.'

'And Lord Jaspar, who was helping her—he nearly ended up dead too, shot at by a silent rifle as well,' said Harry.

'And then there's us trying to investigate it all, and also nearly ending up dead—I guess that's evidence, too.' Arthur was no longer trying to shrug. 'Evidence that this silent assassin we're after is probably working on behalf of this very factory—'

Arthur stopped talking abruptly. There were sounds heading towards them.

Footsteps. Voices.

Chapter Ten

Harry crept silently to the doorway. Earlier, he had lingered in it for some time, keeping watch, listening for any sound of someone approaching. But that was a while ago—for some time now, he had been listening to nothing apart from what Arthur had been saying.

He reached the doorway, and peered out. Along the corridor, two factory workers were standing by the open window. One of them held a metal lamp, and its paraffin flames flickered as a breeze blew under the raised sash. The men's clothes were heavy, their bodies bulky, but their movements were quite quick, one ducking his head out through the window and looking down, the other glancing up along the corridor.

'We shouldn't have left the window open,' Billie hissed in Harry's ear.

'It was so we could escape quickly, if we needed

to,' Harry replied. But he bit down on his lip after speaking.

'How are we going to escape now?' Billie said.

'This factory's got more than one window,' said Harry, looking around the room.

With luck, it'll have more than one drainpipe, too. Harry darted across the office. As silently as he could, he undid the latch of another window, and slid it up. He could hear the mutterings out in the corridor, but no more footsteps, not yet. He looked out of the window, and saw the drainpipe they needed. They would have to clamber along a fairly long ledge and two more sills, but it was possible.

'Keep that file, Artie,' he whispered, pulling back into the office. 'Put everything else back where it was; we don't want them to know we've been here.'

'Of course,' Arthur whispered back, as he gingerly picked up the papers that had fallen on the floor, slid them into the file, and then tucked it into his jacket. Billie darted around him, scooping up the other files he had taken out, dropping them back into a filing cabinet drawer, and pushing the drawer shut.

'Billie, no!'

Harry leapt across the room. Billie had pushed too hard, and the drawer's ball-bearing mechanism was gathering speed. Harry nearly caught it, his fingers brushing against the handle at the drawer's front, but he was too late, and it shot into the rest of the filing cabinet with a clang.

The metal sides shook, the tower swayed and rattled against the wall. The mutterings out in the corridor stopped.

No time at all now. Harry raced to the window, and threw it all the way up. Boots thudded up the corridor, light from the paraffin lamp slanting into the room, and Harry pushed Arthur and Billie out through the window. They leapt away, onto the ledge along the sills, the vital papers bulging in Artie's jacket. *Good.* Harry's fists gripped the edges of the window frame and he pulled himself through, flinging out a boot towards the ledge. But the rest of his body didn't follow.

The factory workers. A hand gripped his jacket, another smothered his face. He tumbled back into the room, and one of his arms twisted up around his back so hard that the feeling drained out of it, leaving only prickling numbness behind. He gritted his teeth as he was bundled out of the room and down the corridor.

'Hold him tight!'

'Spying, maybe!'

'The boss'll want to see him himself!'

They slammed through doors, and thundered down a staircase. The feeling had gone from Harry's arm completely, and hardly any of the rest of his body could move either—too tightly held. The two men hurried down another staircase and past a row of windows which opened on to a shadowy space. Harry glimpsed heavy machines, stretches of conveyor belts, an iron forge. *The factory floor.* He breathed in odours of oil, chemicals, steel, and his tongue curled in his mouth. He saw lines of open crates, and glimpsed the gleaming muzzles of guns, hundreds of them. He remembered the files in that gloomy office room, crammed with neat details of murderous machines. He watched the assembly line blur past, silent and motionless, but waiting to begin its work when the next shift began.

More doors. The men's boots fell silent, falling into a thick rug, running along another corridor. Paintings travelled past, a polished side table, and the smell of the factory floor faded into new odours, of wood and leather. The men turned a corner and Harry was flung into a chair. One of the men kept hold of him, his hand still over Harry's mouth. The other knocked on a door and hurried through.

Harry peered over the hand's pink flesh. His eyes moved around. He was in a waiting room. The rug was thick, the wallpaper flecked with velvet. There were framed photographs on the wall, and he recognized the figure standing at the centre of every one of them. Magwell. Harry saw him posing with important-looking men—army generals, heads of state—shaking their hands, standing next to them in a formal way. He saw him holding weapons, clutching a sophisticated-looking rifle, gripping two pistols. Other photographs showed him holding contraptions that Harry didn't even recognize.

In all the photographs, the scar was plainly visible.

Harry closed his eyes and tried to imagine the man in the pictures but with a cape curling around him, a slanting mask covering the scar. He pictured him, standing on a rooftop.

The door opened. The other factory worker marched through, and Harry was bundled into the room. A fire crackled under a mantelpiece; the walls glowed with patterns of velvet and gold. A mahogany desk squatted at the room's far end, a man sitting behind it. The man leant forward, his face catching the fire's light, revealing that nose, that moustache, that scar.

Magwell.

Chapter Eleven

Logs shifted in the fireplace, spitting out flame. The face lingered in the light, oiled hair shining, shadows curving around the skin. For some time, the man remained where he was, across the desk, broad hands resting on its polished wood, perfectly still. One of the factory workers hurried up to him, bowed, and muttered in his ear. Harry couldn't hear what the words were, but he heard Magwell's reply, a low growl.

'Call the police? No need, fool.'

Those powerful hands remained on the desk, but their fingertips whitened as they took the weight of his body, lifting, leaning forward so that he could inspect Harry more closely. The cloth of his shirt and jacket was soft and expensive, his eyes were cold, but Harry concentrated on the scar. Thick, whitish tissue clung to Magwell's face, as if the whole left side of his head was cupped by a twisted, pale hand. The face turned, glancing across the room, and Harry realized why Magwell had made that remark about the police.

Across the room was another chair, pooled in darkness. Rising out of it, moving forward, was a figure Harry recognized at once.

'Looks like you're not my only visitor tonight, Newton,' Magwell said. 'At least you were expected— can't say the same for this one.'

Inspector Newton walked over, his steel buttons glimmering in the firelight, those eyes glimmering too. But Harry noticed there was something troubled about the policeman, just as there had been a short time ago as he waited by the factory's gate. His body was restless, his heavy shoes kept shifting position, and his eyes darted to the figure behind the desk before moving back to Harry again.

'You!' The policeman glared. 'What are you doing here—'

'Is this one of your Scotland Yard techniques, Inspector Newton?' Magwell's voice blotted the policeman's out, even gruffer and deeper. His accent was an English one that Harry didn't recognize, a growling burr. 'A spy, sent to gather information while you try to distract me with your questioning?'

'What? By no means—'

'Oh really? Police forces often hire street children.

I know they're cheap—clever, too. I've come across it before, in other cities I've worked in.'

'I'm sure you have, Mr Magwell, but that's not what has happened here. I already know this boy—'

'You do know him, then? Recruited him, have you? Been spying on me for some time, has he?'

'Not at all, I simply met him—yesterday it was.' The policeman's head was lowered, his hat gripped in his hands. 'He was poking his nose into the investigation, the curious sort. But as for him being here, I'm as surprised as you are—'

'Really? I'm the one who's truly surprised, I'd say. You told me this meeting was to be entirely between ourselves, *Newton*.'

The bullet casings. Harry could see them resting on a small table next to the desk, their metal catching the light. They were placed on the same pale handkerchief in which Inspector Newton had wrapped them up on the roof. Once again, the circles of letters etched on their bases were too far away to see, but Harry knew exactly what they were. He snatched his gaze away, as Inspector Newton bore down on him, a broad finger pointing at him.

'Followed me, did you? Wasn't I clear enough to you and your friends?'

'Friends?' Magwell watched from the desk. 'A few of them working for you, are there?'

'Not at all, Mr Magwell.' The gruffness vanished from Newton's voice, leaving it strangely shaky. 'This boy was curious about the Rigby Gardens case. He must have followed me as I went about my work, that's all.'

'Careless of you. I expected proper privacy for this conversation, you know that.' Magwell glanced across at the bullet casings on the handkerchief. 'Are you saying it's a surprise to you that some young member of the public should take an interest in the Dame Flora Cusp murder? The whole of London's talking about it. Maybe this boy is someone Dame Flora or her society helped in some way—maybe he's a pupil from one of the Benevolent Orphans' schools.' He studied Harry. 'Well, is it true?'

'Yes, sir,' Harry said, the first words he dared to speak. It was a lie, a simple lie—if Billie had been here, she would probably have thought of something cleverer, but she wasn't, and so it was easier just to echo Magwell's words. *Seems to have worked,* he thought; but then he saw Magwell's eyes narrow, his body move further forward across the desk. The pale hand around the side of his face altered its position as a smile grew.

'Maybe not. The Benevolent Orphans' schools are all in England, and your voice is an American one, I can hear that. New York—I know the accent well, from my visits there.' He studied Harry, and breathed in, as if detecting his scent. 'Your jacket—that weave's different from what you get this side of the Atlantic—one from the Southern States, perhaps. Louisiana, I'd say.' He chuckled. 'You're not the only one who's a detective, Newton.'

'You are most observant, Mr Magwell,' Newton said softly.

'That's what working in the manufacturing business does—makes you aware of such things.' Newton's gaze didn't leave Harry. 'That voice, it's not just American. There's something else in it, too—Eastern European, maybe? Where are you from, boy?'

'Budapest.' *No point in lying*, Harry thought, as Magwell inspected him.

'Ah, Hungary. One of the few places in Europe I haven't visited.' The smile grew larger. 'But I've set up many of the armies that have swept through it, and dealt with the people there. So maybe I have visited it, in my own way. What brings you to London?' The smile vanished. 'What's your business here?'

'Just arrived yesterday, sir. I work in the theatre, a magician's act. It's done well in New York, so I thought I'd try it here.' All perfectly true, and the story rolled easily off his tongue. Magwell appeared to believe it, nodding calmly, and leaning back into his leather chair. 'Did a show last night, actually, at the Trilby Theatre, Constant Lane—'

He stopped. His heart throbbed in his chest. Under his clothes, sweat prickled over his skin. He had noticed something on the far side of the room, a dark shape hanging on the back of a door. *A cape.* Its cloth was dark, but the edge of it was turned, revealing red silk lining, gleaming in the firelight. Harry looked about for any sign of a mask, but there was nothing—*tucked inside the cape, perhaps.* Over by the desk, Magwell was still studying him, but his eyes moved to the cape too, and back. The smile grew again, making the scar shift its position—*that scar caused by testing out his own brutal weapons.* Harry tried to carry on with his story, the business of the theatre, the trick, his innocent magic act, but his tongue froze in his mouth.

He knows it already. He was there. Last night.

'I'll deal with this, Mr Magwell,' said Inspector Newton, a little of his gruffness returned. He stepped forward and stood between Harry and the figure behind the desk. 'No need for you to trouble yourself with a mere boy.'

'Ha! But are you able to deal with it?' Magwell growled. 'You're a man of the law and this boy hasn't committed any offence—just followed you about.'

'He's trespassed on your property,' Newton replied hastily. 'That's an offence.'

'Only if I press charges, which I do not.' The smile

was gone; Magwell glanced at the inspector with contempt. 'I'll deal with this over-inquisitive boy my own way, Newton.'

He was up out of his chair, and walking around the desk. His oiled hair flashed in the fire's light, and Harry flinched as Magwell headed towards him. He glanced at the hanging cape again, and imagined it curling around the tall, muscular figure walking across the room. As the arms dealer bore down, Harry lowered his face, but couldn't help noticing Newton on the other side of the room, looking pale with alarm.

'Calm yourself, Newton,' Magwell said. 'I only want to talk to him.'

And he stared down at Harry, crouched below him on the rug.

'An illusionist, a magician, eh? You Eastern European folk are fond of magic, I know. Maybe that's where you get your curiosity from—you like finding out how tricks are done, do you? The flick of a wrist, a sleight of hand and all that. Maybe you thought you'd try your hand at puzzling out this new mystery, the one about whatever's happened to dear Dame Flora Cusp?' The deep voice spat out the words. 'But I'm warning you, boy. Don't become an innocent caught up in something you don't understand.'

Harry kept his face lowered, staring down. He

concentrated on the flecks of spit that had landed on the rug, thrown from the arms dealer's lips as he spoke Dame Flora's name. He concentrated on the muscles around his own eyes, cheeks, and jaw, keeping them still, controlling his expression. Magwell bent down, and that smile drew closer.

'Innocents. I've got used to their suffering, conducting my trade. Accidents in my factories, mishaps during transportation, and then there's the work of the weapons themselves, waging war across the globe. Revolutions crushed, governments flung down and lifted up once more—all in a hail of lead and iron from my factories. Stay out of the way, that's all I ever tell people, and that's what I'm telling you now, boy, loud and clear. Stay out of the way, whatever your interest in this business might be.' Magwell rose back up. 'Sensible advice, don't you think, Newton?'

Harry caught sight of the policeman again, who seemed unable to control his expression at all, confusion flickering freely, and a touch of fear too, entirely out of place on those fierce bearded features. Newton glanced between Harry and Magwell, and even edged forward as if to intervene, but then shuffled back.

'Indeed, Mr Magwell,' he said quietly.

'Then let's carry on with our private meeting, you and I.' Magwell swung away, gesturing at the factory workers who had been gripping Harry's arms through-out. 'You there—throw this boy out.'

The hands tightened, dragging Harry out of the room. He saw that tall figure sweeping round to the other side of his desk; sitting back down in his chair. He saw the cape on the door, the turned-back edge of red velvet. He saw Inspector Newton, slowly returning to his own chair, and sinking down into it.

And he saw, still resting on the handkerchief on the little side table, those three bullet casings, glinting in the light.

Chapter Twelve

Harry crashed onto the cobbles. The factory workers had thrown him hard, and he only just flung out his arms in time. They took the force of his fall, and then he spun himself in a somersault, so that his body hit the unflinching stones as evenly as possible. He made sure he cried out, and lay there looking as crumpled as he could, while he waited for the workers to leave.

The gate clattered shut, but he waited a little longer before springing up and darting into the nearest alleyway, in which he had seen two pairs of watching eyes, even as he was being thrown through the air.

'Harry, are you all right?' Arthur asked.

'They could have seriously injured you, hurling you onto stones like that!' Billie said.

'Just got a bit mucky, that's all,' said Harry, brushing off his jacket. But he was shaking as he stood up, and the story shook too, as it raced from his trembling lips. Harry led them down the alleyway, telling them everything, about the meeting with Magwell, the appearance of Newton, the bullet casings—and he went back earlier as well, explaining about the figure on the roof and his slanted mask, and how he had thought it was no more than a hunch earlier, not worth distracting them with, but not now. He noticed that Arthur and Billie were no longer checking his body for injuries, but were staring at him, following every word that came from his mouth.

They crossed a street and clambered over some railings into a small park. Harry dropped down on the other side, and checked around to see if they were being watched. He couldn't see anyone so led the others over to a nearby bench surrounded by bushes. They sat down. Arthur and Billie were no longer staring at him, but looked off into the darkness of the park instead, their faces furrowing with concentration.

'Newton could have been there for a perfectly ordinary reason.' Billie was the first to speak. 'Like we said when we saw him, Harry. He could be conducting his investigation, and so he decided to confront Magwell with the evidence of the bullets found at the scene of the crime and ask for an explanation. That's what policemen would do, all over the world.'

'Doesn't fit with how nervous he was,' said Harry.

'Or with what I saw up on the roof, opposite 24 Rigby Gardens. He was deliberately not letting the other policemen have the bullets, I'm sure of it.'

'And it seems suspicious to me anyway, taking the bullets to show Magwell.' Arthur frowned. 'Valuable evidence would normally be kept locked up in a police station. Taking that evidence along to the very person who might be incriminated by it, in the place where they work—that makes no sense.'

'So what are we saying—that Newton's somehow tipping Magwell off about the fact they've been found?' Billie asked.

'Friends in powerful places, not unusual for big businessmen,' said Arthur. 'Particularly not for ones in the murky business of trading arms. Remember what Dame Flora said in her letter—about him using powerful connections to get round the ban on selling weapons to Ravelstan? I wouldn't be surprised if he had useful friends in the police force as well. Friends more powerful than Newton—his bosses, his masters. I'm afraid that's something else policemen do all over the world, sometimes—not investigate a crime properly because the person involved is rich and powerful.'

'Rich and powerful—and downright nasty in this case,' said Billie. 'Are you sure it was Magwell up on the roof, Harry?'

'As sure as I can be. The slanted mask, remember? And then there's the cape, too—I saw it on the back of his door.'

Harry drew his jacket close around him. It was the middle of the night, and a cold wind crept through the park, finding its way through his clothes. But he shuddered even more at the thought of the flickering light of the fire in Magwell's office, and all it had revealed. Most of all, the threatening face of Magwell himself, drawing close. *Stay out of the way . . .*

'Why did he let Harry go?' Billie muttered. 'If Magwell really is behind the attacks on the Benevolent Orphans, and the one on us, then why didn't he do something? When Harry was right in front of him—'

'Because Newton was right in front of him, too.' Harry's hands bunched into fists. 'Even if he has got a special arrangement with the police, he wouldn't be able to . . . Not right there—'

'More to the point, he wouldn't be able to do anything if Newton locked Harry up, either, kept him nice and safe in some London police station. Which is why he was so very firm about not pressing charges, about not wanting Harry arrested.' Arthur said. 'No, he wants Harry out and about on the London streets with his two friends. So he can—'

The park seemed to grow darker. Harry wondered

if one of the gas lamps nearby had flickered out, and he scanned the inky shapes of the nearby bushes, checking for movement. He listened for the tiniest sound, a body rustling through leaves or a twig cracking under a boot. He gathered his arms around himself, trying to stay warm. He glanced at his friends. They were trembling too, and clouds of frozen breath stole from their mouths.

'Of course, Magwell could have been serious,' said Arthur, quietly. 'About people being perfectly safe if they stay out of his way.'

Harry tried to make out his friend's face. He had turned it away slightly, and the dark made it hard to see. Billie had gone perfectly quiet. Harry saw one of Arthur's hands disappear into his coat pocket, and slowly lift out the thick metal tube containing the explosive powder from the grenade.

'Enough to blow up a dressing room, and the rooms all round it.' Arthur stared at the tube. 'And the thing is, that was only his first go. At trying to get rid of us, I mean. I wonder what else he's got in his factory there?' He looked back across the park in the direction they had come from. 'It's not as if we're up against just anyone, that's what I'm thinking—'

He fell silent. Billie wasn't saying anything either, and for some time they just sat on either side of Harry.

The night wind seemed to have icy fingers, and they slid into his clothes, snatching away any tiny remaining warmth that might have collected in their folds. He shivered.

'You're right, Artie, it's not just anyone we're after.' It was Billie who spoke, in the end. 'But it's not just anyone we're trying to help, either.'

She took Arthur's hand, then grabbed hold of Harry's hand too, and pulled it together with Arthur's. Warmth gathered in that tight bundle of fingers and palms.

'If it's Magwell, then he won't stop at Dame Flora,' Billie went on. 'He's already tried to murder Lord Jaspar. Remember what the Benevolent Orphans said at their press conference—that nothing would stop them carrying on Dame Flora's work?'

'Then nothing'll stop Magwell either,' said Arthur, nodding. 'He'll keep going, for as long as they get in his way. He'll destroy them completely, and that'll be the end of all their charitable works. Hospitals, schools, campaigns for famine relief, everything.'

'A whole society of folk who've come from nothing, and now just want to help others.' Billie talked faster. 'And that's what we're about, too, like you said, Harry. That's what we did in New Orleans, back in Manhattan . . .'

'Maybe Mr James did mean something by it? The stuff he said on the train at Southampton, about how this mission was particularly suitable for us,' Arthur said. 'He wanted to prepare us, to make us realize how important the Benevolent Orphans society is.'

'How it's worth saving, no matter what.' Billie smiled. '*The rescue of others is a triumph for all*—it really could be our motto. Just like we said before back at the theatre—'

'A few seconds before the grenade came down the chimney, nearly killing us all.' Arthur swallowed nervously. 'Not that that makes any difference, obviously.'

With his spare hand, Arthur held up the metal tube. He pushed it back into his pocket, and tapped it until it was out of view. Then he moved his hand across to the others that were gathered on Harry's knee, and gripped it, quite determined. Harry felt Billie's hand tighten too, and he thought of what his friends had said. Several times he had opened his lips, only to find that one of them was already saying what he was thinking, word for word. But at last they had fallen silent, and so he spoke.

'So that's decided. Dangerous or not, we're carrying on,' he said. 'And to start with, I think the Benevolent Orphans might like to have a look at that file about the Ravelstan weapons contract we discovered, don't you?'

Chapter Thirteen

Silver domes rested on the white-clothed table in the St Pancras Hotel breakfast room, up on the building's top floor. Out through elegantly curved windows, the London skyline could be seen, bathed in morning light. A waiter lifted the silver domes, revealing platters of eggs, sausages, bacon, and devilled mushrooms, and he served up plates of the food, which he placed in front of Harry and his friends, and in front of Sir Julian Elkins-Ford, the one member of the Benevolent Orphans whom they had managed to contact so far.

'Eat, eat, dear children!' The spindly gentleman waved at the plates of food with one hand, as he wound up a telephone by its crank with the other. 'You have suffered the most terrible sequence of shocks—you must fortify yourselves.'

'Thank you, Sir Julian,' said Arthur, as he carried on leafing through the contents of the file from

Magwell's factory, a small Russian dictionary now in his grip. 'Although actually I'm a bit busy trying to translate these documents.'

'Come on Artie, force a bit down,' said Billie, spearing an egg with a fork. 'It's been a busy night—we need the energy.'

But she clearly didn't have much appetite either, just nibbling at the egg. Arthur took a bite of toast but nothing more, and Harry felt the same, abandoning his mushroom. It had been a busy night, but an anxious one too, and his stomach felt tight with nerves. After the conversation in the park they had managed to sleep a little on the bench, but it hadn't been easy, each of them taking turns to stay awake and watch for any sign of the assassin. Then when morning had come, there had been more nervousness, as they hurried to the shops to get Arthur a Russian dictionary, ducking between doorways in case they were seen. They continued to the St Pancras Hotel, where they faced more difficulty trying to persuade the hotel staff to put them in touch with the Benevolent Orphans.

It was only by chance that Billie happened to notice Sir Julian emerging out of the hotel's caged lift, dressed in another expensive suit with various new handkerchiefs protruding from its pockets, and with a morning newspaper under his arm. They had run across, introduced themselves as three children from a local theatre who had become interested in the Dame Flora murder and then, to grab his attention, they had shown him the components of the dismantled grenade. Less than a minute later, they were sitting at his table up on the top-floor dining room, telling him the story, and that was where they had been for the last half hour, as an extremely flustered Sir Julian sent telegrams and made telephone calls to the other Benevolent Orphans to summon them to the hotel.

'That's everyone on their way.' He hung the telephone's earpiece on its iron hook. 'I don't suppose you need to make any telephone calls yourselves, do you? It's a new-fangled contraption, but I can show you how to use it.'

'It's all right, we don't need to call anyone, and we know how to use it anyway; they have them at some of the theatres we work in, particularly in New York,' said Harry.

'Yes, we're actually familiar with quite a lot of contraptions,' said Billie. 'This one for example, eh Artie?'

She nudged Arthur, who was trying to translate another Russian document from the file, and pointed at the components of the grenade, which were arranged on a plate as carefully as the waiter had placed the bacon, egg, and mushrooms on the platters. Sir Julian went pale, and lowered a forkful of egg from his lips. He wiped his mouth with another handkerchief, one with tropical fish stitched around its edges.

'Indeed—a fearsome device! Thank goodness you were courageous enough to continue your enquiries. And thank goodness you came to find me this morning—I and the other Benevolent Orphans are all due to catch a train in just a couple of hours in order to attend Lord Jaspar's Paris Conference for World Peace. I wonder if we will be able to attend it now, after your extraordinary discoveries—ah, here comes Lady Brewster. You must share those discoveries with her!'

The dining-room doors had swung open and the elegant lady bustled through, a taffeta dress swelling about her, her hands clutching a large carpet bag out of which numerous bound manuscripts bulged. She hurried towards them, out of breath and pink with exertion. Arriving at the table, she collapsed into a chair.

'I came as soon as I received your telegram, Sir Julian! I was in the middle of packing for the eleven forty-five from Victoria!'

'As was I, Lady Brewster—but these children's remarkable discovery changes everything, does it not?'

'Indeed it does!' The flushed face swung towards Harry and his friends. 'Tell me all!'

'Well, the best place to start is with this grenade,' said Harry, but didn't get any further, because just then the doors swung wide open again, and in stumbled another Benevolent Orphan, Professor Roger Winterskill, straggly-haired and with that pink-tinted monocle jammed in one eye. He too was red-faced, breathless, and clutching a telegram as he stumbled across the room and slumped down at the table. Harry opened his mouth to start again, only for the dining-room doors to swing open another time, and the final member of the Benevolent Orphans, their elderly leader, came tottering into the room, his frail body hunched over his ivory-handled walking cane.

'Ah, Lord Jaspar!' Sir Julian leapt up and guided the invalid towards the table. 'Thank goodness you could come so quickly!'

Lord Jaspar tottered on, his walking cane's tip jabbing into the dining hall's floor, and Harry saw those sunken eyes, that pain-stricken face. The old man was wearing a new, clean jacket and there was no sign of blood, but the material around his wounded arm was already crumpled from being gripped. Sir Julian helped the old man on his journey until at last he reached the table, and sank into a chair. His walking cane clattered to the floor, and his worn-out gaze fell on the grenade components on the plate, next to the salt cellar.

'Tell all!' Those sunken, tear-filled pools stared at Harry and his friends.

Harry did. Billie joined in, and even Arthur lifted his nose from the documents and the Russian dictionary to add a few remarks. The whole story poured out again; their first investigations at 24 Rigby Gardens, then the business of the grenade, followed by the experiments and research at University College, and how it had led to Magwell's factory. Then Harry gave them a full account of his meeting with Magwell and Inspector Newton. When he had finished, Harry looked around the table at faces wide-mouthed with shock. Sir Julian had heard the story before, but even he looked dazed, and the others appeared to have fallen into a trance, from which they were emerging only slowly. Professor Winterskill struggled to lift a coffee cup with a shaking hand, Lady Brewster's face had gone almost white and, next to her, Lord Jaspar's pain-filled eyes stared on, a hand edging towards his wound.

'Ernest Magwell. Can that really be the identity of our attacker?' Sir Julian dabbed his forehead with another handkerchief, one with galloping horses on it this time. 'It would make perfect sense. Dame Flora was indeed deeply committed to her work at the hospital in Ravelstan.'

'Not just that.' Billie pulled Dame Flora's letter from the file. 'She was taking Magwell on directly, threatening to expose the fact that he's trading arms illegally. Bring him down, that's what she says.'

'Indeed, how like her that was,' said Lord Jaspar. 'Kindly, but determined. Not only her! I must have been earning Magwell's wrath—I have devoted my life to seeking peaceful solutions to conflicts, remember, and the conference we are about to attend in Paris seeks specifically to address that awful Ravelstan war from which, it turns out, he profits. I was setting that conference up when the assassin attempted to murder me—oh, it is all clear now!'

'What a miracle you survived.' Professor Winterskill gripped his quaking coffee cup as firmly as he could, but it was shaking faster, rattling against the saucer and spilling everywhere. 'But what cruel tragedy that Dame Flora did not!'

'What cruel tragedy we *all* face, if we fall into this monster Magwell's clutches!' Lady Brewster cried. 'Have we not all vowed to continue each other's charitable works? Which would certainly, and quite rightly, include continuing the work regarding Ravelstan, and thus bringing down Magwell. He will have all of us in his sights, all!'

'Not to mention these poor children. He has

attempted to blow them to smithereens merely for taking an interest in this affair—a monster!' Lord Jaspar clutched his arm, a tear rolling from one of his sunken eyes. 'But we must allow this to change nothing, Benevolent Orphans! *The rescue of others is the triumph of all.* Each of us has experienced danger and hardship before—we were born penniless orphans, were we not?'

'And yet we rose from those difficulties and survived to do good!' Sir Julian's fist, still clutching his galloping-horses handkerchief, struck the table, making the cutlery, plates, and pieces of grenade leap. 'We must do the same now. For the sake of our noble cause, we must fight back with all our strength!'

'But how?' Lady Brewster held a bottle of smelling salts to her nose, looking queasy. 'These children have supplied us with vital information, but acting on that information might be rather hard—'

'Might be lethal, not to put too fine a point on it.' Sir Julian's shoulders lowered. 'Ernest Magwell is a powerful enemy. I say that as someone who works in the manufacturing trade; as a businessman, his ruthlessness is well known. He is a man who has crushed princes; entire armies have been swept from the battlefield by his vile machines. He is not to be crossed—'

'I do not care!' Professor Winterskill cried above

the rattling of his cup, blinking as coffee flew into his eyes, splashing into one directly, spattering the pink monocle jammed in the other one. 'He has murdered one of our members, and attempted the murder of another, and of these children—we shall do battle with him, Benevolent Orphans! I am a legal scholar—I shall do battle using the force of the law!'

'That might be tricky,' said Lord Jaspar. 'Because you heard what young Harry said about this Inspector Newton fellow being involved, didn't you?'

'Of course, but we must not let that deter us!' said Sir Julian. 'If there is corruption in the London police force, we must shine a light on it. If we must do battle with powerful men, so be it.'

'So say I!' said Lady Brewster. 'We owe it to our cause, and we owe it to these children. They have risked everything, breaking into an arms dealer's factory in order to unravel the mystery—'

'I'm not sure we *have* quite unravelled it, actually,' Arthur's voice cut in.

He was still holding the Russian dictionary, a thumb amongst its pages. In front of him, the file was open, with its various documents covered in Russian handwriting. With his spare hand, Arthur had lifted up one in particular, and he was peering at it with particular puzzlement. It was another letter, but very different from Dame Flora's; it was in Russian, with a large eagle printed at the top of it. Arthur glanced at it, and then at the dictionary, and then back at the letter again.

'Sorry it's all taking so long,' he said. 'But Russian verbs never decline the way I expect—it's very confusing. Although it's not as confusing as what the letter actually means . . . '

'Tell us,' said Harry, but he hardly heard his own words, because almost everyone around the table was saying similar things, leaning forward, their gazes fixed on the tweed-suited boy with the Russian dictionary, and on the letter in his hand. Harry peered at the letter, noticing as he did so, that Professor Winterskill's cup had gone entirely still.

'It makes things a bit more complicated, that's all,' said Arthur. 'This letter's from the king of Ravelstan's government, War Division, you see. When I first saw it, I thought it was about the contract between the king and Magwell, for the weapons used against West Ravelstan—discussing some technical matters, maybe. But the thing is, now I've declined all those verbs, it seems this particular letter isn't really about the king of Ravelstan *buying* arms from Magwell at all—it's a letter cancelling his order.' He picked the letter up again, scanned it as if hoping he had missed something, but shrugged. 'It informs Magwell that the king's ministers have found another supplier prepared to sell them arms illegally, one in Berlin—and they're cheaper. So they're cutting off his contract halfway through. Magwell, it turns out, isn't actually selling weapons to the king of Ravelstan—not since a couple of weeks ago, which is when the letter was sent.' He put the letter down again. 'Sorry everyone, I thought I should mention it.'

Harry looked around the table again. Lord Jaspar and Lady Brewster were exchanging confused glances; Sir Julian gripped the edge of the table with a fist. Professor Winterskill reached across for the letter. He did this with one hand, Harry noticed, the other holding his cup and saucer quite steadily.

'That's new information, certainly. A shame I don't read Russian,' Professor Winterskill said, his scholarly air returned. He shrugged, and passed the letter back. 'But it doesn't necessarily change anything. Magwell may have lost this contract with the Ravelstan king, but that doesn't mean he won't be angling for another.'

'Indeed, he's a businessman first and foremost,' Sir Julian interrupted. 'And businessmen don't like to take no for an answer. He'll have written straight back to the king's ministers, offering a cheaper price. There's probably another letter in the file proving just that.'

'He could have offered a lower price, or superior weaponry—both standard business tactics. So he would still have every reason for wanting to get rid of Dame Flora and, indeed, me,' Lord Jaspar said. 'Remember the other information we have—not least the involvement of Inspector Newton. Why else would a senior police officer be tipping Magwell off about evidence if something underhand wasn't going on?'

The Benevolent Orphans huddled, and muttered amongst themselves. Harry heard them discussing bits of the story he and his friends had told them. Billie was holding the letter, looking at it sceptically, while Arthur earnestly sorted through more of the documents, and flicked through his dictionary.

'Collect yourselves, fellow Orphans!' Lord Jaspar tapped a sugar bowl with a spoon. 'We cannot be surprised that this matter remains unclear. Our investigators are mere children, after all.'

'That's true.' Lady Brewster fretted. 'We are expecting too much of these intrepid youngsters. I in particular have become quite carried away with the thought that they would come to our rescue—you all know my weakness for using child heroes to turn a story; my novels are full of them.'

'With good reason, dear Lady Brewster,' Professor Winterskill nodded. 'These young heroes have made an excellent start. It is up to us to use our power and influence to continue the work—ironing out every detail of the case against Magwell, who is most certainly behind it in some way, one confusing letter or not.'

'Yes, we must unmask him, for the sake of our cause! Remember that, Benevolent Orphans!' Sir Julian lifted his arm, his handkerchief in his fist; it fluttered defiantly. 'We may have sprung from sad beginnings, but we have risen from them to do nothing but good! And nothing must endanger that, nothing!'

'*The rescue of others is a triumph for all!* Never let those words fall silent!' Lord Jaspar clutched his arm harder; traces of blood could be seen, starting to soak through. 'Now, we are due to catch the train to Paris at eleven forty-five, and I believe we should do that—our cause must continue. But we have a couple of hours to discuss this further, not least regarding how to finance an extensive investigation—'

'Yes, an excellent idea,' Professor Winterskill said. 'My young friends, will you excuse us for five minutes, while we discuss money matters? The hotel staff will show you somewhere to wait. I hope you don't mind.'

'Not at all. We'll have a think about how to carry on investigating,' said Harry.

He rose from his chair. Arthur gathered up the

bits of grenade, and Billie shuffled the papers back into the file. Professor Winterskill stood up and led them across the dining room, his straggly hair fluttering over his collar, his monocle firmly in his eye. He muttered instructions to a waiter, and then bowed neatly as Harry and his friends filed out. Harry looked back and saw the professor marching back towards the Benevolent Orphans swiftly, determinedly. Then he and his friends followed the waiter down the corridor, and out through a pair of glass doors into a small roof garden, high up amongst the surrounding buildings.

The waiter hurried away, and Harry wandered into the garden. A large potted gingko tree rose in the garden's centre; a wrought-iron table stood on a square of chamomile lawn; a bench was nearby. Harry, Arthur, and Billie sat down on the bench. The morning air was still fresh, and Harry breathed it in, trying to clear his thoughts. He looked around at the nearby rooftops and towers. He listened to the sounds from the street below, of crowds, of rattling carriages and carts.

'It was the right thing to do, telling them,' Billie said.

'But what exactly did we tell them?' Arthur said. 'In the end, I'm not sure—oh, if only I'd been able to translate a bit quicker.'

'We told them what we knew. Not our fault if

something unexpected turned up at the last minute.' Harry patted his friend's shoulder. 'And you heard what they said—they still think it's Magwell, don't they?'

'It *is* Magwell,' Billie said. 'It's too much of a coincidence, him being involved with the king of Ravelstan's horrible war—even if the deal didn't quite go through. That letter is just one bit of evidence, Artie.'

'Not very strong evidence, either,' said Harry. 'Like Sir Julian pointed out, there could easily be another letter in that file, saying the contract's back on.'

'That's true.' Arthur fished out his dictionary again. 'I'd better get translating again.'

'And another thing—just because the King's ministers said they could get the weapons cheaper, that doesn't mean they're telling the truth,' Harry mused. 'Maybe they discovered Dame Flora was going to make a fuss. Maybe that's why the king of Ravelstan pulled out. If Magwell found that out, he'd have more reason to want her dead than ever—could be pure revenge for wrecking the deal.'

'I'd definitely better get translating,' said Arthur, reaching for the file, which Billie had stuffed back into her smock. Then he stopped. 'Wait a minute— what are we doing out in the open? We're targets, remember?'

Harry's head swivelled left, then right. He saw something, and froze.

'You're right, Artie—broad daylight, too.' Billie was starting to stand up. 'We've been so busy thinking, we forgot. Better get back inside—'

'It's too late for that,' said Harry, grabbing his friends' arms.

Like them, he had casually wandered out into the roof garden, absorbed in thoughts of their investigation. He had briefly forgotten the danger they were in, but he remembered now as he looked across to the building opposite and saw that familiar figure, a distant shape up on the roof.

That cape, that distinctively arranged mask. *Magwell*, he thought.

He was holding a rifle, a long slender one with a distinctive barrel-shaped muzzle. He was lifting it up, and aiming it directly at them.

Chapter Fourteen

Harry jumped up onto the top of the bench's back. It tilted under his weight, and slammed backwards onto the roof behind it, tipping Billie and Arthur off it.

'What are you doing?' Billie scrabbled at the concrete.

'I'm meant to be the nervous one, not you!' Arthur sat up. 'It's actually pretty safe here. It's still inside the hotel really and—'

One of the bench's slats split in half, next to his head. A bullet ricocheted off the roof's brickwork and smashed through a nearby window. The garden echoed with the sound of shattering glass, and Harry peered through the remaining slats at the figure on the next roof, who was reloading his gun.

'Magwell!' Billie saw the figure. 'The cape! The mask! It all fits, like you said, Harry—'

'That rifle, it's firing silently. It must be the one I

saw the designs for back in the factory,' cried Arthur, as another wooden bar shattered, a bullet whirring past. 'The one he used on Dame Flora!'

'I'll distract him,' said Harry, preparing to spring. 'Wait until I've gone, then run for the doors.'

He sprang out from behind the bench. He heard his friends shout after him, but he was too busy racing for the large potted gingko tree in the middle of the garden. The corner of his jacket kicked up, and he saw a bullet hole straight through the pocket. He ducked, leapt in the air, and dodged from side to side, and it worked because he heard another bullet whistle past, missing him, shattering another window. Another dodge, and Harry was standing behind the gingko tree's trunk, as the garden echoed with the sounds of tumbling glass. He peered round to see Billie and Arthur scrambling through the doors into the safety of the hotel. Arthur tripped, but Billie managed to hold him up, while flinging an arm back in Harry's direction.

'Harry! Watch out!'

Harry's head swung left. The shooter had moved further along the roof across the street, and had a clear shot at him around the gingko's trunk. Harry shuffled around the tree, even as it shuddered with another bullet, perfumed gum and splinters flying from its side. He saw the figure move along the roof, ready with a new angle. The rifle snapped open, the figure reloaded. Harry heard bullets click into place, the rifle snap shut.

He saw, a few yards away, the round garden table, made of iron.

He dived under it and tilted it up. The table's iron-work was moulded into leaves and curling vines, and it vibrated in his hands as a bullet clanged off one of the leaves. Through the dense metalwork, he saw the figure on the roof reloading again. A long-range rifle, easily capable of finding a target through these intricate metal curls and loops . . .

But not if they're moving.

Gripping the round table's edges, he rolled it towards the hotel doors on the other side of the garden. Another bullet clanged off the iron, jolting the table off course, but he steadied his grip, rolling it on, weaving past plant pots and the tipped-over bench and some fragments from the shattered window panes, keeping the flowering metal between him and the figure on the roof. Another bullet struck, and the whole table shuddered with a musical chime, and spun out of Harry's hands completely, but he was close enough to the doors. He leapt through them, and looked back at the table, which was still spinning, rotating on its edge like a huge coin until it slammed onto the ground.

'Did you get hit? Anywhere?' Billie's hands raced over him.

'It's all right, there's no blood, only this.' Arthur held up the side of Harry's jacket with the bullet hole through it, frayed threads round its edge. 'Close, though.'

'So much for that garden being still inside the hotel.' Billie's voice was tense and flat. 'A rooftop firing range more like and—'

'Heavens above! Children, are you all right?'

The Benevolent Orphans were tumbling out of the dining room at the other end of the corridor. It was almost impossible to tell them apart, their bodies were moving so fast, but Harry saw Sir Julian's flailing arm, Lady Brewster's frilled dress, and Lord Jaspar's legs, tangled up with his walking cane. He made out different voices too, howling out of the muddled blur.

'A miracle! You have escaped, but how?'

'The police are on their way!'

'We heard the windows shatter! Then a servant ran in and told us—he saw it all from a window!'

'A lethal long-range rifle, just as you warned us! A sophisticated weapon—Magwell shall not be allowed to get away with this!'

Magwell. Harry swung back to the doors leading to the roof garden. He looked round them, and saw the caped figure on the other roof. He was striding towards a fire-escape at the building's side, the rifle slung across his back. Shouts could be heard from the streets below.

'C'mon!'

Harry grabbed his friends. He pulled them along the corridor, straight through the tangle of Benevolent Orphans, who were still spilling out of the dining room. His friends seemed slow, and Arthur was even pulling back, but he dragged them to the main hotel staircase, and raced down it, floor by floor, until he reached the pillared lobby. It was a blur of activity: porters running, guests shouting, clerks shouting into wind-up telephones. Harry raced on, and plunged into the spinning glass and bronze of the hotel's revolving doors.

'We're going out there? Are you mad? He'll shoot at us again!' Billie was in the compartment behind him, her face pressed against the glass.

'No—he's on the run,' Harry said. 'Listen to what's going on—people saw him, didn't they?'

'He can still take a shot at us if he's on the run!' Arthur was on the other side of the glass with Billie, struggling to stay upright as the doors spun.

'There's no other way of finding him,' Harry shot back. 'Look, we'll split up, search in different directions, that'll make it harder for him—'

He toppled out onto the hotel steps, his friends falling out behind him. Arthur was still unsteady; Billie was supporting him, but she was unsteady herself, her arm around Arthur unnaturally tight. Together, the three of them glanced in every direction, and then stared straight down the steps, at the men heading directly towards them.

A tight band of policemen, with Inspector Newton at the front.

Chapter Fifteen

Heavy blue-coated bodies surrounded them, hemming them in. Harry tried to push through, but hands gripped him, and spun him round. He saw Newton's face, flushed with anger. The policeman glared at Harry, and then up at the St Pancras Hotel.

'Might have known we'd find you here. Came to find the Benevolent Orphans, did you? Found out they hold their meetings here? Thought you'd carry on your poking about—'

'We're not poking about, we're trying to help them, aren't we?' Harry shouted back. 'You should be trying to help *us*—he tried to kill us, shot at us from that roof up there.' He couldn't point, because the policemen were holding his arms, so he jerked his head towards the building across the street. 'Magwell—'

Newton's arm shot out, and his bulky hand sealed off Harry's mouth. It covered half of Harry's face too, but one of his eyes could still peer between the policeman's thick fingers, and he saw Newton's face flush even deeper, redness glowing through the pale strands of his mutton-chop beard. The other policemen shifted uncertainly at the sight of their master's sudden anger, but the hands holding Harry remained firm.

'I *am* trying to help you, fool!' Newton spoke again, and his voice was different, a desperate hiss. 'Tried to help last night, when you were out of your depth. You do know what danger you're in, don't you? What I've got to do if—'

'How can I know?' The hand had moved and Harry could speak again. 'When you keep trying to stop us? Or do I mean cover things up—'

'Shh Harry!' Arthur cried, but there was no need, because Newton had done the job for him, covering Harry's mouth back up with his hand. The inspector glared, and then swung round to the policemen nearest to them, and muttered to them. Harry saw their faces become as confused as Arthur's and Billie's, and he struggled harder, trying to shake away Newton's hand, trying to shout out to the crowd of passers-by who had gathered by the hotel steps. He kept scanning the surrounding streets, the nearby buildings, for any sign of that masked figure, that fluttering cape.

'Officers, release those children immediately! In the name of the Benevolent Orphans! They are merely trying to help, and have risked their very lives in doing so!'

Sir Julian Elkins-Ford was bursting out through the revolving doors. Behind him, the other Benevolent Orphans could be seen in the spinning glass. Newton watched Sir Julian stumble down the steps towards him. Then he spoke to his men, his voice firm, steady, and loud enough to be heard by anyone around.

'Arrest these children for their own safety, and for interfering with the due course of the law.'

The policemen pulled Harry down the steps. He struggled, but the blue-coated arms were sturdy. Across the street, he saw two more policemen waiting by a horse-drawn carriage, a heavy black box with iron doors and tiny grilled windows in its sides.

'A Black Maria!' Arthur gasped. 'That's what they use here for transporting criminals—'

'Shame they haven't found any proper criminals to put in it,' Billie said. 'Newton just wants us out of the way!'

'That's right! So we don't tell anyone what we know about him and Magwell!' Harry spluttered, as the policemen bundled them into the carriage's dark insides. The arms released them, the iron

142

doors clanged shut and everything went black. Harry crouched on the rough floor, waiting for his eyes to adjust, breathing in the Black Maria's odours, of iron, of wood, of sweat. A key clattered, and he saw the glimmer of a keyhole. Above him, fingers of light slid through the barred windows, and he jumped up and looked through them. Back on the steps of the hotel, the Benevolent Orphans were confronting the policemen, Sir Julian waving his arms imploringly, Lady Brewster pointing one of her rolled-up manuscripts in the direction of Harry and his friends. But the policemen simply stood there, arms folded, shoulders set, obeying their master's orders. Harry looked around for Newton, but he couldn't see him, lost in the muddle of blue-uniformed bodies.

'Harry! Look!'

'It's HIM!'

The darkness throbbed with Billie's cry. Harry saw the silhouettes of his two friends' heads, pressed against the grilled window on the other side. He pushed his head between them, and stared through the bars. A short distance away from the carriage, ten yards at the most, an alleyway ran between two buildings.

Lingering in its shadows, the man in the cape.

He stepped forward. He was level with the street, and the light fell on the edge of his cape, but not his masked face. Harry saw the rifle strapped across his back, but concentrated on the figure's right hand, which was inside the cloak, pulling something out, throwing it towards the Black Maria. The figure stepped back into the alleyway, fading into the shadows. The object, small, black, metal, rattled along the pavement towards the carriage.

'Another grenade!' Harry stood on tiptoe, trying to peer down at whatever it was, as it rolled nearer and nearer.

'Maybe we'll be safe—this thing's made of solid iron and wood, isn't it?' Billie said. But she was gripping the bars so tightly that her knuckles were almost white.

'It's not a grenade! We're not safe, not at all! I recognize it from the factory papers—I saw one as I flicked through!' Arthur clung to the bars too, his whole body shaking as the object disappeared from view, rolling under the carriage. 'It's an incendiary device!'

Harry dropped down and put his ear to the thick wooden floor. Faintly, he heard the sound of the object rattling to a halt on the stone cobbles directly below.

'An incendiary device— What's that— What does it do—' The words seemed stuck in Billie's throat, and she spat to get them out.

'There are various kinds.' Silhouetted against the

bars, Arthur tore at his hair. 'If I remember, this particular one is packed with a flammable oil with a timed detonation device—'

'What does it do?' Billie forced the words out again.

'It sets fire to things!' Arthur flung himself against the door.

A thud, from under the carriage. The floor lurched, and Harry looked up at the barred windows on either side of him.

Already, smoke was curling up past the bars, and they were flickering with the light of flames.

Chapter Sixteen

Horses screamed and the prison van hurtled forward. Harry tumbled onto the wooden floor, bowling into Billie and Arthur. Hooves thundered on cobbles, and the whole carriage raced along, shuddering up and down.

'The horses! They're trying to get away from the fire!' Billie staggered up, and managed to peer through the grille.

'They can't get away! The device has set fire to the carriage and they're attached to it by their reins, aren't they? They're just making it burn faster—the wind's fanning the flames, look!' Arthur pointed at the other barred window, and the licking flames, even brighter.

'Harry, pick the lock! Quickly, before the smoke gets too thick and suffocates us!' Billie cried. 'Or before the flames burn us to death—Magwell wasn't taking any chances with this one!'

The carriage tilted, careering round a corner,

throwing them all against the side. Harry heard the crackle of fire, and smoke filled his mouth, thick and bitter. Tiny flames leapt between the thick planks of the floor, dancing around the soles of his boots. He trod through them, trying to keep his balance as the carriage gathered speed, and his fingers scampered in his pocket, searching for the little bent nail he kept there. Harry toppled against the side again, and the Black Maria's iron frame burned through his jacket, as the heat crept through it. He stumbled on towards the keyhole, bright with the fire on its other side.

'Faster, Harry!' Billie's cry was hoarse with smoke.

'I can't—we're shaking about too much.' Harry tried to push the nail in, but it bounced off the key-hole's edge.

'Just try—it's the only chance we've got.' Arthur clung to him, gripping his arm. At least the flames make it easier to see.'

It was true, the flames were leaping even higher between the planks, and the racing carriage flickered with their light. Harry pushed in the nail. He gripped the edge of the door, trying to keep himself steady. He angled the nail against the lock's metal insides, trying to work out the position of the springs and levers, but then pain seared into his finger and thumb, as the nail's metal filled with heat.

'It's no good,' he gasped. 'The heat from under the carriage is travelling up through the iron—it's reached the lock, it's gone into the nail.' His eyes watered as he tried to keep his grip tight. 'I can't hold it—'

Another scream of the horses, and it was as if a giant hand had picked the carriage up, and thrown it. Harry's stomach lurched, and he flew upside-down through the darkness, his head by the flaming floor. He saw the street flashing past the bars of the window, then the London sky, then the street again, as the burning carriage spun and rolled and twisted.

'The horses, they've broken free!' Billie yelled. 'The fire must have burnt through their reins and—'

The Black Maria thudded to a halt. Harry collapsed in a heap, Billie and Arthur landing on top of him. The carriage had landed more or less upright, but it was tilted to the side, and the flames licked up one of its walls. Harry searched for the keyhole in the smoke. But the nail was gone from his finger and thumb, even though they still stung with pain from its heat.

'My pick, I've lost it. It could be anywhere—we'll never find it.'

'We'll find something else.' Billie tore through her pockets. 'Anything long and thin—you look too, Artie—'

'It's not that easy, is it?' Artie searched his pockets,

but his hands were shaking uncontrollably, and kept getting stuck. 'It's got to be the right shape for this lock, and it can't be metal either or it'll heat up like the nail did and—'

Harry grabbed his friend's hand, holding it still. In the light of the flames, he had seen his hands brush over a particular pocket, which bulged with a particular shape.

'Let go, Harry! I can't search if you won't let me move!' Arthur was nearly sobbing.

'Sorry.' Harry loosened his grip. 'But that's Magwell's grenade, down in that pocket, yes?'

'Yes, but you can't use that—none of its parts are the right shape for poking, not long and thin—'

'I'm not going to be doing any poking.' Harry delved in the pocket, ripping its stitches. 'Which bit was the charge—this?'

He held up the small metal tube, sealed at the top. Light from the flames danced on its surface, and on Arthur's and Billie's faces too, each flicker revealing a new expression, more terrified than the last.

'Yes, that's the charge.' Arthur could hardly speak. 'Good point—once the flames reach that, and melt the tube, it'll go off. We're not just going to get suffocated and burnt alive, we're going to get blown up as well—'

'Wait a minute, Artie.' Another flicker, and a hint of hope on Billie's face. 'Maybe we change the order of that. Maybe we do the blowing up first, then we might not have to bother with the other bit—that's what you're thinking, yes Harry?'

'It might work,' said Harry.

He made it back to the door. The flames were leaping almost a foot high, the smoke made it impossible to breathe, but he managed to crouch down. His hands dripped with sweat, so he wiped them on his jacket, his shirt, his hair. Then he started unscrewing the tube.

'Careful.' Billie was next to him, a hand on his shoulder. She was trying to hold him steady, but her hand was shaking. 'One slip and—'

'I know.' The tiniest lick of flame and the contents of the tube, which had nearly blown up several rooms of the Trilby Theatre, would blow up everything inside a locked London prison van instead. *But that's not going to happen*, Harry told himself, as he took off the lid, and held the tube perfectly steady.

Just a little. In the lock.

He placed the rim of the tube by the keyhole's edge. As the flames leapt by his feet, he tilted the tube, and watched a trickle of the green powder fall into the lock's insides. Billie's hand slid off his shoulder, and she sunk to her knees. Arthur had flattened himself against the carriage's far side, rigid with fear.

'That's enough,' whispered Harry, righting the tube, and immediately screwing the lid back on. He turned to Arthur and took hold of his tie. His fingers unknotted it, and drew it from his friend's sweat-soaked collar. 'It's not valuable, this tie, is it?'

His friend tried to open his mouth, but no sound came out. There were no sounds coming from Billie either, no wisecracks, no stories, nor anything else. Harry dipped one end of the tie in the flames, making it catch light, and he saw his friends' soot-covered faces, streaked with tears. He leapt back to the lock, stuffed the unburning end of the tie into it, leaving the other end dangling below, flames travelling up it. Grabbing his friends, he huddled with them as far away as he could, their arms weaving around each other as they watched the tie.

'Sorry it's burning so slowly.' Arthur loosened his sodden collar. 'I'm afraid it got a little damp with perspiration, what with all the excitement.'

Then he flinched, and turned away, as the flames speeded up, burning up the rest of the tie, and vanishing into the keyhole. Harry turned away too, shielding his face, and Billie buried her head in his jacket. The Black Maria flashed with light. It was as if another giant hand had reached in, this one surrounding all three of them, and squeezing hard. All Harry could hear was a high-pitched whining in his ears and all he could see was smoke.

He waved his arms, trying to clear it and saw the remains of the door. The keyhole was gone. The whole lock was gone, a ragged circle of light in its place. Harry flung out a leg, kicked the door open, and heard it tear off its hinges. He toppled through, pulling his friends out with him, and dragged them away across the street, before collapsing onto the cobbles.

Chapter Seventeen

Harry sat up, his eyes stinging. Fire had taken hold of the Black Maria completely, a column of flames and smoke reaching into the sky. Tears trickled down to his lips, tasting of smoke. He blinked, and saw Billie and Arthur, sprawled in the gutter, smoke rising from their clothes. He made out a crowd of onlookers gathered on a nearby pavement, too stunned to move.

He stumbled to his feet. He closed his eyes, rubbed at them, and forced them open again. And even though the stinging tears clung to them, he held them open all the same. Because he had seen something move in the blur, a little away from the crowd, further down the street.

The flutter of a cape, vanishing into an alleyway.

His eyes blurred again, the tears too thick to see through. He rubbed them, looked again, and the man was gone. But he ran towards the alleyway, a ribbon of blackness running up between two buildings. Reaching it, his hands gripped the cool brickwork edges. He shook away the smoke-filled tears.

Down at the alleyway's end, the cape billowed, just in view. Then it vanished around a corner.

'Was that him?' Billie stumbled up to Harry. 'Magwell?'

'I can't see . . . ' Arthur was further away, rubbing his eyes. 'My ears . . . They're ringing from the explosion . . . '

Harry's ears were also ringing. His legs were weak, his hands clung to the alleyway's walls, his clothes were heavy with sweat after the terrifying moments in the burning prison van. But Billie and Arthur were in an even worse state, Billie just about managing to stand, Arthur sinking back onto the cobbles again, gasping as smoke curled from his clothes. Billie ran back to help him, but tripped as she did so, and fell.

'You wait here . . . ' Harry said. 'I'll follow him. I'll track him down . . . '

He plunged into the alleyway. The walls raced past him as he hurtled along it, leaping over dustbins, splashing through puddles. At its end, he saw it branched off in three different directions, a maze of crooked passageways leading into the dark. He heard footsteps behind him, and the clatter of a dustbin.

Billie was stumbling up the alleyway, her arm round Arthur, who was tottering beside her.

'Go back! It's too dangerous!' Harry yelled.

'Can't let you go alone. What if he tries something else?' Billie gasped back.

'Yes, we're here to help, Harry.' Arthur stared about in the gloom. 'But are you sure you'll be able to find him? Which way did he go?'

'I don't know,' said Harry, but then pinned himself and Billie to the wall as a brick next to him shattered into orange dust, a bullet howling into the dark. Harry saw the caped figure, down at the end of one of the passageways, vanishing into the gloom again, the long-range rifle gripped in his hands. He vanished around another corner and Harry gave chase, his friends following behind.

'It's definitely Magwell, has to be,' Harry said. 'The rifle, the grenade, the fire-bomb—who else could get their hands on all his top-secret weapons?'

'Of course it's Magwell!' Billie cried. 'But how are we going to find him like this? He'll shoot us for sure!'

'These alleyways, they're too dark, too narrow!' Arthur spun around, looking in every direction. 'Maybe he knows them, maybe he's leading us into a trap—'

He ducked as another brick shattered, another bullet whined. Harry spun round to see the caped figure down at the end of another passageway entirely, one leading off into a different part of the maze. He was reloading his rifle, lifting it to his shoulder, and Harry tugged his friends into a doorway just in time, as another bullet screamed past.

'It's too late,' wheezed Arthur. 'He's cut us off, hasn't he? He's between us and the way back to the street!'

'Artie's right.' Billie's hand tightened on Harry's shoulder. 'We're trapped.'

She pushed herself as far into the doorway as she could, her back pressed against the door, one side of her face crushed against it. Arthur was desperately trying to keep himself hidden too, his boots braced against the doorstep. Smoke was no longer rising from their clothes, the tears on their cheeks had dried, but Harry saw new tears glint in their eyes as they shrank back, waiting for the next bullet. Spotting a crack between the bricks at the doorway's edge, Harry leant forward and peered through it. Down at the far end of the alleyway, a few rays of light slid in from the open street. Standing in those rays, blocking them off, was the caped figure, his rifle snapped open, his hand in a pocket, fetching bullets.

The hand stayed in there, Harry noticed, for some time.

'We might be all right,' he whispered, pulling back into the doorway.

He listened as carefully as he could for the click of bullets pushed into place, the rifle snapping shut— he remembered the sounds of the rifle's reloading, drifting across to him as he huddled behind the roof garden's gingko tree. But now, even though the assassin was so much nearer his prey, none of those sounds could be heard at all.

'Harry, what are you doing?'

He stepped out of the doorway and stood there in full view of the man in the cape, who was still down at the passageway's end, the rifle still open. A hand hovered near it, and it would be the quickest of moves for the rifle to close, for a finger to squeeze its trigger, for a bullet to flash up the passageway towards him. But the man in the cape just stood there, his gaze moving between the gun and Harry, and back to the gun again.

'He's got no bullets left,' said Harry. 'He's used them all, up on the roof garden, here in these alleyways . . . '

The figure was gone again. The cape furled, the rifle clattered against a wall, and the man vanished into the gloom. Harry cursed himself for not moving sooner, but he decided to make up for it, racing all the way down the passageway to where his hunter had stood. Crouching down, he picked up the rifle and saw two bullet casings lying on the ground, the results of the assassin's final shots. Gleaming in their bases was the word *Magwell.*

'Why leave the rifle?' Arthur took it from Harry's grasp.

'No good to him with no bullets,' said Billie.

'But it's valuable, and it's evidence.' Arthur examined the rifle's long sight.

'Heavy, isn't it?' Harry said, glancing down the various passageways. 'Long, and awkward to carry. Doesn't want it slowing him down.'

'But Magwell—you said he's pretty big, pretty strong?' Arthur frowned. 'He wouldn't have any trouble carrying a rifle—'

A dustbin rattled down at the end of the passage to Harry's left. Harry ran on.

'Maybe he's not Magwell,' he said.

'Not Magwell? Who else could get hold of the weapons? You said it all added up!' Billie ran beside him.

'That was before, when I met him at the factory. I saw the cape on the back of his door, and he was the same height and shape—but like Artie says, why would a strong man not be able to carry a gun?'

Another spidery junction. Harry's neck twisted as he searched for any sign of movement.

'But if it's not Magwell, who is he?' Billie's hand clutched his arm, the fingers digging in.

'We should go back—at least if it's Magwell, we know who we're dealing with,' Arthur stumbled up.

'How can it be anyone worse than a ruthless arms dealer, responsible for making the world's most deadly weapons?' said Harry.

'I don't know, but that's what this investigation's been like,' said Billie. Her grip tightened, and she was pulling him back. 'Every step of the way, it's turned out way more dangerous than we could have ever thought.'

'We've got to get out of here.' Arthur pulled at Harry. 'Don't worry, we'll find out who he is, but not here, not this way, hunting him through dark alleyways when at any moment he can—Billie?'

A whispering breeze, by Harry's ear. He had seen something too, a tiny blur in the dark. He swung round, and saw Billie sink onto her knees, her eyes fluttering shut. As she fell he saw the tiny dart, the length of a matchstick, protruding from her neck.

'Billie!' Arthur tried to hold her up but her limbs sprawled. 'Harry, I told you, we've got to get out—'

Another whispering breeze, another blur in the dark. A dart was quivering in Arthur's skin, on his left wrist. His legs gave way, and Harry tried to lower him gently down, but had to duck as another dart flew in, and struck him glancingly on the arm.

It bounced off. But it had scratched him; his legs started to shake and he leant against the wall. Suddenly the complicated web of passageways was gone, and all Harry could see was just one, and the caped figure advancing steadily along it. He saw the figure hunch over some kind of pistol, reloading. *Grab it.* He was stumbling up the passage, lunging from side to side in the hope of throwing off the assassin's aim. The pistol rose, but Harry was nearly upon him, reaching for the gun.

The dart shot straight into Harry's hand, sinking to its hilt. His arm swung to the side, pulsing with pain, throwing him off balance. Harry stumbled into the man and then dropped onto the alleyway's cobbles. Numbness flowed up his arm, and spread into the rest of his body. He saw the caped figure, who had been thrown against the wall, the mask knocked away.

It can't be. Harry glimpsed the face, but his vision blurred, and his thoughts dissolved.

Harry's eyes flickered shut, and his body softened onto the hard stone.

Chapter Eighteen

Iron beams. They jutted at angles, a pattern of bolted-together lengths, stretching off as far as Harry could see. An icy breeze cut against his face and he heard faint sounds of the city. Looking down, he saw water, the surface of the river far below—cold grey waves, edged with white.

The chime of footsteps on the iron beams. Harry tried to move but his arms and legs were tied to a girder with tightly knotted rope. He managed to turn his head, and he saw him, the cape furled to one side, the mask down.

It can't be.

'Needlessly complicated, needlessly brutal, all of this. But you left me no other way.'

Lord Jaspar. Those sunken eyes contemplated Harry, but the kindly expression had fled. All signs of the wounded arm had gone, and so had the ivory-handled walking cane. Instead, the old man swung spryly through the bridge's iron bars and landed on a walkway a few feet away. A black metal box waited there, wires sprawling from it, and Lord Jaspar crouched over it.

'I tried to dispose of you neatly, I really did.' He fished a spanner from his suit. 'A simple grenade ought to have been powerful enough, but you dodged it. A volley of rifle fire when you were in the roof garden, followed by a carefully aimed incendiary device when you were in the Black Maria—you dodged those, too. And you carried on dodging as you pursued me through the alleyways, until I had run out of bullets, forcing me to use the tranquillizer darts instead. But what was I to do with your drugged bodies, which would awake and ruin everything at the most critical moment of my plan? With some effort, I loaded those bodies onto a cart, covered them with sackcloth, and transported them out onto the Victoria Railway Bridge—which is where you find yourself now, about to face death by the most unpleasant means of all.'

He rose from the box and bent over Harry, his elderly hands tightening the ropes with surprising quickness and strength. *The rope trick*—Harry remembered it from the Trilby Theatre, and from all the other times he had performed it, and he tried to clench his muscles, draw in a breath. But the drugs made him weak, and it was too late anyway, because the ropes were already too tight, digging into his body, cutting under his ribs, making it impossible to move.

'Attempting your little deception?' Lord Jaspar's face was inches away. 'I was in the audience that night, and I witnessed that ingenious escape. But I've worked it out—you make your body as big as you can, then let the breath out and so on. Simple, really.' He pulled a rope even tighter, forcing another gasp of air from Harry's lungs. 'But hard to do when tranquillized.'

'But I saw you . . . ' Harry tried to remember. 'In the corridor when we were running from the roof garden . . . I saw you and the other Benevolent Orphans . . . Your walking cane . . . '

'You saw Winterskill,' Lord Jaspar said. 'The poor fool had a shaking fit due to the stress; you may have witnessed him spilling all that coffee. He took a pill, which calmed it, but it resurged after you left for the roof garden, pretty much took him over. The hotel staff provided him with a spare walking stick—you saw him, not me.'

The ropes were like the iron girders of the bridge, rigid, unflinching. The knots were perfectly positioned too, not a single one of them anywhere near Harry's reach. His hands were locked by his waist, held firm by a knot around his wrists. Harry struggled, pulled, pushed, but the ropes dug even deeper, burning and pinching his skin. Harry detected tiny vibrations running up them, and he jolted his head round, making out the shapes of Billie and Arthur tied right behind him, the same ropes winding round the same thick iron beam. They were just waking up, and the ropes were vibrating with their feeble struggles.

'Lord Jaspar . . . ' Billie's voice was dull and heavy. 'But the Benevolent Orphans . . . He's one of them . . . '

'Where are we . . . ' Arthur slurred. 'What's going on . . . '

Harry managed to crane his head a little further round. His friends were at the very edge of his vision, but he saw their faces turn pale with fear as the drugs released their hold.

'But it can't be him!' Billie struggled. 'He was the first one the assassin attacked! In Paris—wounded his arm . . . '

'Except his arm's perfectly all right. He m-must have faked the wound,' Arthur stuttered. 'Made up the attack to s-stop anyone suspecting him of carrying out the murder of Dame Flora himself, not to m-mention the attempted murders of us.'

'But why?' Billie said. 'Why kill Dame Flora, who

devoted her life to the Benevolent Orphans, when he was a Benevolent Orphan himself—'

'For goodness' sake, is that not perfectly clear?' Lord Jaspar was back by his wire-festooned box, but his voice rang off the bridge's iron. 'Really—perhaps I didn't need to worry about your plucky little band investigating after all. Please don't tell me I have wasted my time with my efforts to dispose of you.'

Harry's head ached with the drugs. The complicated pattern of iron beams dissolved into a blur, impossible to work out, but he forced his eyes to focus, and it came into view again, the intricate, slanting shapes. He tried to bend his fingers upwards, to touch the knots around his wrists, hoping to probe them, find a weakness. But his fingertips didn't even brush them, too far away.

'Lord Jaspar—he's the leader of the Benevolent Orphans, but maybe he's different from the rest of them,' Harry hissed to his friends. 'Maybe he wants to interfere with their work. I don't know why—perhaps he doesn't agree with it, perhaps he wasn't orphaned at an early age like the rest of them—'

'Oh I was orphaned! I can assure you of that!'

Lord Jaspar released the wires. They slid from his fingers and sprawled madly about as his wrinkled face lifted, and those eyes stared out of their sunken pits;

his lips arched, revealing yellowed teeth. Harry sensed more vibrations down the ropes, and guessed Billie and Arthur were flinching at the sight; he couldn't help flinching against the iron girder too.

'Orphaned children, such innocent creatures,' Lord Jaspar snarled. 'They suffer terribly and so, if they prosper later in life, what could be more natural than to turn their attentions to the sufferings of others—how many times have I had to listen to the Benevolent Orphans witter on so. What a relief, to at last be able to say out loud what I truly think about their feeble philosophy! *The rescue of others is a triumph for all!*' Those gentle words spat from his lips. 'What if there was a different sort of orphan, just one perhaps, who chose to deal with his suffering differently—right from the beginning? A particular orphan, at a brutal orphanage not far from here, who decided one day long ago not to sit there and suffer, but to get his hands on a little bit of extra gruel, by whatever means he could?'

He was working on the wires again. They spooled as his fingers jabbed at them with renewed force. He kept looking up, his eyes studying Harry and his friends.

'A swift scoop of my spoon, when the orphan next to me wasn't looking. The smallest act, but conditions were harsh, and that tiny extra amount of food burnt usefully inside me—too bad about the girl who went without. Yes, from the earliest age, poor orphan that I was, I decided to fend for myself however I could, and it didn't take long to work out that, far from worrying about the sufferings of others, I would have to *cause* that suffering in order to get what I desired. I stole more gruel, grew stronger, and then I turned my attention to other thefts, pilfering the few precious items my fellow orphans possessed: trinkets, items of clothing, keepsakes from deceased parents, anything that could be resold. Once I was nearly caught, but a swift planting of evidence meant that another orphan, entirely innocent, was dragged off by the orphanage master for brutal punishment. I waited outside the room, listening to his cries—and I reflected on the skills I had learnt, the skills that would go on to serve me so well in life, all the way up to my infiltration of the Benevolent Orphans in these last few years. The double-crossing and defeat of poor innocent children: that was how it all began.' His eyes settled on Harry and his friends again, and the lips around the yellow teeth smiled. 'You three youngsters are bringing back happy memories.'

He picked up the box and crouched down next to them. He tied the box to Harry, Arthur, and Billie, looping ropes around the iron beam as well. Harry watched the old man's fingers as they tightened the knots, and saw how fast and strong they were. He tried to struggle again but his body hardly moved, and then Harry froze as he noticed something about the wire-covered box, tied to him and his friends. Letters were stamped into it, arranged in a familiar circle: *Magwell.*

'So you've been taking their money?' Billie was trying to keep her voice steady. 'That's it, isn't it? All this time you've been pretending to be in charge of the Benevolent Orphans, but like you stole food and trinkets from other orphans at the orphanage, you've been secretly stealing money from your own organization!'

'Embezzlement, that's the official term for it,' said Lord Jaspar, and the sound of the word was like a sweet drink being sucked up a straw. 'Half a million I've made, over the years.'

'But Dame Flora found out.' Arthur's face was white with fear, but he was thinking, too. 'That's what must have happened. She discovered what you were up to. The whole thing was nothing to do with Magwell at all—'

'Not quite nothing to do with him.' Billie interrupted him, her gaze fixed on the black box tied to them, and on the letters on its side. Then she looked back up at Lord Jaspar. 'You used Magwell's weapons, didn't you?'

'Indeed I did.' Lord Jaspar pulled tight a final

knot, and stood up. 'Nimble thinking—it was worth pursuing you after all.'

He flicked a switch on the box. A steady ticking started echoing out of it. Harry could feel the ticking too, new vibrations creeping down the taut ropes binding the box, him, and his friends to the bridge.

'Yes, I stole the weapons,' Lord Jaspar continued. 'I had been aware of Dame Flora and her growing inquisitiveness about the society's finances for some time, and had puzzled what to do about it. Frankly, she provided her own solution, thanks to her unceasing concern for wretched West Ravelstan, and its unfortunate collision with Mr Magwell's business interests. An idea for how to dispose of her came to me, and I simply visited Mr Magwell disguised as an ordinary investor in his enterprise. Amounts of money were discussed, but no agreement was ever reached—nonetheless, on one of my visits I took the opportunity to rifle his desk, discover the key to his store of secret weapons, and help myself. Such skilful thievery.' A smile. 'To think it all started with a spoonful of gruel.'

So horribly calm, Harry thought. Lord Jaspar had moved away from them and was leaning on one of the bridge's girders as he told his story, the wind fluttering through his clothes. Harry looked down at his own clothes, held firm by the ropes, and he saw that they were dark with sweat. His heart pounded in his chest, his muscles shook, and his fingers scrabbled pointlessly, thanks to the meticulous tightness of Lord Jaspar's knots. *Impossible.*

'You used his rifle to kill Dame Flora,' said Billie, 'and you deliberately left evidence, knowing that would make everyone suspect Magwell was behind it, didn't you?'

'Yes, the bullet casings . . . ' Arthur added. 'You left them there.'

'The bullet casings, and everything else,' Lord Jaspar said. 'I did everything to lay suspicion on Magwell—I wore a cape similar to one I saw on the back of his office door, I wore a mask that slanted as if covering his scar—'

'And it worked,' Arthur said. 'The bullet casings, when Newton found them . . . '

'Inspector Newton, the perfect investigator for my crime—if only you three could have been a little more like him,' Lord Jaspar snapped. 'I knew that Magwell had the most senior police officers in his pay, Newton's bosses included. An understandable arrangement for an arms dealer, given the difficulties of the trade. He has a protected status, in other words, and so what did Inspector Newton do when he discovered apparent evidence of Magwell's involvement? Why, he took it straight to Magwell himself, warning him of it, promising him that the investigation would never be pursued, that his force would simply announce it as unsolvable in the interests of everyone concerned.'

Newton. Memories flashed through Harry's mind. The police officer sitting in Magwell's office, angry yet afraid; his command to arrest them on the hotel steps; the slamming of the Black Maria's doors. But the memories were fleeting, vanishing almost as soon as they arrived, as his mind filled with nothing but fear. It was taking over his body, too, making his muscles weak and the hairs lift on his skin. Vibrations from the ticking box kept creeping down the ropes. He remembered the trick at the theatre, and how he had carefully chosen which knots to undo first. He stared desperately down at the knots surrounding him now. *Every single one of them out of reach, and no way of breathing out . . .*

'Inspector Horace Newton: methodical, predictable, a bloodhound trained to follow the trail I had left, and then to quietly bury it, also in a canine fashion.' Lord Jaspar smiled again, briefly. 'But then there was you, investigators of a very different kind. I watched you from a nearby window while you sneaked onto the roof of the building opposite Rigby Gardens—just over-curious children, I thought at first. But I followed you anyway, watching you as you arrived at the Benevolent

Orphans' press conference, asking your cab driver for any possible information about you—then I doffed my disguise and returned to my role of poor wounded Lord Jaspar.' He delved in his velvet jacket and plucked out a leather bag, steadily dripping a red liquid, with various rubber tubes attached. He tossed it away.

'I watched you listening so keenly at that conference, then I followed you to the theatre where you played that night, and noted with concern your remarkable skills of trickery, skills that clearly indicated you were a threat. No mere children, no mere journalists either, I thought—and so, with the help of another of Magwell's weapons, I made an attempt on your life. An attempt that failed!' He glared at Harry, stepped across and checked the tightness of the knots once more. 'Powerless, I was forced to watch as you went about your work, investigating Magwell, breaking into his factory, stealing his files, probing my careful arrangement. For a while it seemed you had just decided it was Magwell, too—but then there was the work of your polylingual friend!'

'Polylingual? What's that mean?' said Billie.

'Fluent in lots of languages.' Arthur forced down a frightened swallow. 'Although it's Russian he's talking about, and I'm not actually fluent in that—'

'Fluent enough!' Lord Jaspar seethed. 'Every recklessly translated word of that letter threatened to expose my plan, whether the verbs were correctly declined or not! You had alerted the Benevolent Orphans' attention to the possibility that Magwell might not be involved, and I knew further investigation would only lead to more discoveries, more exposure. Are you surprised that, as soon as Professor Winterskill suggested in all innocence that you step out onto the roof garden, I immediately made my excuses, stumbled with my walking cane to the next room, then tossed away said cane and made my way to the roof of the next building, from where I launched a series of deadly attacks on you using more of the weapons I had stolen—weapons of which only one more remains.'

He nodded at the ticking box. The numbness spread up Harry's fingers. Sensation was fading from them, but his mind had never felt more terribly alive; every one of Lord Jaspar's words was like a knife, stabbing into his thoughts. Harry's heart throbbed against his ribs, as the box ticked on.

'All things must come to an end and, thanks to your interference, my Benevolent Orphans enterprise must come to an end—too many questions are being asked,' said Lord Jaspar. 'But I have prepared for this moment. A couple of months ago, I persuaded my fellow society members to insert a powerful clause in their wills, stating that on their demise all their wealth would instantly transfer to the society. Those clauses will be activated in precisely seven minutes' time.' From his pocket, he lifted a fob watch on a chain. 'It is currently eleven forty-two. You recall that the Benevolent Orphans are due to attend the Paris Peace Conference tomorrow? They have just boarded a train at Victoria Station, which will depart at eleven forty-five. I have sent a message informing them that I have been sadly delayed, and so I shall not be with them, in the dining carriage, when the train rolls out of Victoria Station; nor will I be with them four minutes later, at eleven forty-nine, when the train crosses this bridge and this device, one of Magwell's most powerful bombs, explodes, destroying this portion of bridge, the train, the Benevolent Orphans and, of course, the three of you, along with all the information you might have gained. No, I will not be anywhere nearby—I will be making my way south to Portsmouth, where I plan to board the next steamer to Argentina, once the entire wealth of the Orphans has transferred into my name.'

Silence, apart from the ripples of the river, the faint sounds of the city, the ticking of the box. Harry craned his head round, and glimpsed Arthur and Billie, their mouths open. His body slumped—a sight that seemed to cause Lord Jaspar considerable delight.

'As I've said, the years of never expressing my true thoughts at those endless meetings of the Benevolent Orphans have taken their toll. Not seeing them meet their fate today is a further frustration.' The old man lifted a shoe onto the iron walkway. 'But seeing you learn of yours makes up for that. You are rather like the Benevolent Orphans, you see. Whether you are actually orphans, I am unsure, but you are clearly children who have ended up on your own, separate from your families. And, like the Benevolent Orphans, you have a certain compassion for others—why else would you risk everything to carry out this investigation? *The rescue of others is a triumph for all*—it could almost be your motto too, and you offer proof of the Benevolent Orphans' great belief, that hardship at a young age can often result in people keen to do good to others.' He repocketed his watch. 'Although that didn't happen to me.'

The rescue of others is a triumph for all. Harry stared at the old man, his wrinkled lips, his yellowed teeth. How strange to hear those words spill from that horrible mouth, the words that had echoed through this investigation ever since it began.

'Anyway, it's eleven forty-five now,' the old man continued, staring off towards the buildings at the far end of the bridge. 'Porters will be blowing their whistles, the train will be chugging out of the station—it always departs on time. I have checked.'

Harry could hardly hear Lord Jaspar. His head was too full of the Benevolent Orphans' motto, and he wasn't hearing it from those wrinkled lips anymore, but from the Benevolent Orphans themselves, their voices whispering in his thoughts. Gentle Sir Julian, passionate Lady Brewster, Professor Winterskill too—he saw their faces as they proclaimed their noble motto. He closed his eyes and saw those gentle folk taking their seats on the train, ordering cups of tea perhaps, entirely unaware of what lay ahead. *And all the other people on the train, too.* He opened his eyes again.

'Four minutes to go,' said Lord Jaspar, pocketing his watch and turning back to Harry, his friends, and Magwell's bomb, securely tied around the iron beam. 'And then the train will be at this very spot. Goodbye, young friends.'

The rescue . . . Others . . . A triumph for all . . .

'To think, it all started with a spoonful of gruel,' Lord Jaspar said, and he climbed off through the iron beams.

Harry said nothing. He was too busy thinking about the beginnings, the very beginnings, of a plan.

Chapter Nineteen

11.45. Harry scanned the nearby buildings. He made out several clocks, one on a church, another on a tower, all showing the moment of the train's departure had arrived. *And four minutes after that . . .* The ropes cut into his body, the knots as hard as fists, but he didn't struggle. Instead, he put all his effort into turning his head, straining round his neck as far as it would go, so that he could get the best possible look at his friends, and every single knot holding them.

'I can't breathe,' Arthur gasped. 'I've never seen ropes pulled so tight!'

'Course they're tight—he saw us do the rope trick, didn't he?' Billie spluttered.

'And he saw us getting out of the Black Maria and the roof garden too; he really won't be taking chances this time—' Arthur tried to struggle, but his body hardly moved. 'Help us, Harry!'

Their voices shook with fear. It was as if all their efforts to keep it under control had given way at once; Billie's teeth chattered, and strangled gasps came from Arthur. Harry concentrated on turning his head even further, until he saw them fully. Their clothes were damp with sweat, their fingers were bleeding from wild panicky efforts to pick at the ropes. Wild, panicky efforts—*and that's the problem.*

'Artie—you've tried to undo your knots, yes?'

'Of course!'

'What about you, Billie?'

'Are you crazy? Of course I have! Every one I could reach!'

'And I've been trying to undo mine,' Harry said, his voice slightly steadier. 'That's just it—we've been so scared, we've each been concentrating on our own knots. Not each other's knots, not any of the other knots and ropes either.'

His eyes swivelled right to the edge of their sockets. He studied the knots and ropes securing them, criss-crossing their bodies, looping around the bomb and the bridge's girder. He hunted for the slightest point of weakness, a slack rope, a loose knot; there was none. They were mercilessly tight, as tight as the ones around him—there was no way his friends could release a breath, or relax a muscle, to make a little extra space. *But what about another way of doing it?* He scanned Arthur's body, his clothes, but couldn't see what he needed. Then his eyes moved to Billie, the pockets of her smock, and he saw something at the very edge of his vision.

A corner of pale card, sticking out of a pocket. The file from Magwell's factory, filled with papers, including that Russian letter. The file might be half an inch thick, maybe more. It was stuffed inside Billie's smock, and a rope ran across it, taut. The plan kept shaping itself in Harry's mind.

'What, Harry?' Billie had noticed him looking at the corner of card.

'Pull it out,' Harry said. 'It should slide out, and it'll release some space when it's gone—it'll be like when I breathe out, doing the trick.'

'Pull it out how?' Billie fought against the ropes. 'I can't reach it!'

'Arthur can,' said Harry. He had calculated the distance. 'Just about. If he uses his teeth—'

Arthur was already trying. His head had lunged forward, and his lips brushed against the corner of the file, but missed. He lunged again, the muscles of his neck stretching, and his teeth caught hold. He gritted them, jerked his head upward and the file jerked upwards too, sliding out of Billie's smock. The rope over Billie's body, where the stuffed file had been, loosened, and one of the ropes around Harry, connected to it somehow, loosened too. *Just like I'd breathed out . . .*

'The train!' Billie cried.

The scream of a steam whistle ripped through the air. Arthur's head swung round, the file dangling from his teeth, and its papers slithered out, spiralling in the breeze. Beyond the far end of the bridge, billows of steam rose over the city's buildings, each dirty blast growing closer. Harry's eyes swept across to the clocks of the London skyline—they were pointing at 11.46 now. *Three minutes left . . .*

But the ropes were definitely looser. *And at least I'm not dangling upside-down like in the trick.* Wriggling, Harry managed to slide an elbow free. His hands could move more freely too, and he pushed them forward, and dug his fingers into a knot near Billie's hip. It was the loosest one he could see, and his nails jabbed into its fibres, finding their way.

Something gave, deep in its twisting strands. A loop pulled free. The knot slid apart, and the ropes loosened a little more. Billie's left hand sprung out, and started tugging at ropes, while Harry focused on another looser-looking knot, by Arthur's shoulder.

'There's no time, Harry!' Arthur struggled. 'There's twenty-three knots left, the ones I can see anyway—I've counted them. The ones holding us to the bomb, and then there's more holding the bomb to the bridge . . . '

'There's time, Artie.' Harry's voice was quite steady. 'We just have to do them in the right order, that's all.'

The right order. Harry's voice was firm but he couldn't stop his fingers from shaking as they scrabbled and pulled. He hadn't realized the exact moment when the plan had slotted together completely, but it had done so, and it was in his mind, every terrifying detail of it. He had counted the knots too, worked out which ones to do first. *First Arthur's and Billie's, setting them free. Then the ones attaching the bomb to the bridge. Only then, in the time that's left, do the others, and somehow get the bomb away from the train* . . . Fear swept through him, but he tried to use it as he had always done, to concentrate his thoughts. The ropes around his wrists were looser now, and his hands carried on working, pulling apart a knot by Arthur's knee, another by Billie's neck. His friends were almost free, and he saw from their faces that they were starting to work out his plan, too.

'What about your knots, Harry? The ones attaching you? Do those—you'll be able to work faster after that. I'll help.' Billie scrabbled at his knots.

'No, I'll do those later; they're the easiest ones,' he lied. He concentrated on the knots tying the bomb to the bridge's girder.

'That's not true. Lord Jaspar knew you'd be most trouble—he tied your knots hardest of all.' Arthur was looking at him, and his face was turning paler as the plan became clearer. 'You need to start work on them soon, Harry, and when I say "soon" I actually mean pretty much now because—'

'The train, Harry! The train!'

The train was coming. Another shriek and Harry saw steam billow up from the buildings just next to the bridge's north end. An engine thundered, drawing nearer; Harry's hands tore at the last of the knots securing Billie, and then moved back to the ones securing the bomb to the iron girder. They were tighter, almost as tight as the ones tying him to the bomb—none of which had been untied. He pushed his fingers into the rope, and winced as a nail snapped clean off. But he kept going, because the plan was perfectly clear in his mind now, and the sound of the train made it clearer still.

'The rescue of others is the triumph of all,' he said. 'Lord Jaspar's wrong about the Benevolent Orphans. They're not weak, they're strong—way stronger than him.'

'What do you mean? They're on a train, about to get killed!'

'No they're not,' said Harry. 'They're going to

survive. And the work they do, that's going on, too. And it's all because of that motto of theirs—they're not the only ones who believe in it, are they?'

'What are you talking about?' Billie spluttered.

'Us—we've risked everything,' continued Harry. 'This investigation has got more and more dangerous, but we've kept going with it—'

'Of course we have! But what's that got to do with it?' shouted Billie.

'We broke into Magwell's factory together, we escaped from the burning Black Maria together.' He looked at Billie, and then at Arthur. 'You followed me into the alleyways even though we were being shot at—'

'We wouldn't let you down, Harry.' Arthur's face flickered with uncertainty. 'And we wanted to help the Benevolent Orphans—'

'Exactly! That's the sort of thing we do. We're just like the Benevolent Orphans, like we've said.' Harry kept going. 'And that's why, when this bomb explodes, it's not going to be anywhere near the train. It'll be down at the bottom of the river and—'

'Harry! You're not going to—'

She's realized. Arthur had realized too, and both of them were trying to undo his knots, the ones that attached him to the bomb. *But there isn't enough time.*

He concentrated on the knots that needed, that truly needed, to be done first—a few last ones attaching his friends to the bomb, a few more tying the bomb to the bridge.

'There's no other way. No way we can undo all the knots and get the bomb away from the bridge as well. Not unless I—'

'Don't do it!' Billie yelled. 'Let me do it—I'll get rid of the bomb!'

'No, I will.' Arthur's voice was quieter, but as desperate. 'Leave me attached, Harry, I'll jump with it, I'll try to get free as I fall—'

'That's what I'm saying. You, me, all three of us— we'd take any risk to help each other, to help other people, too.' Billie's eyes were wide with shock. Arthur was frantically fumbling at the knots tying him, Harry, not his own. A new knot, a hard, bulky one, lodged in his throat. 'It's just this time, it's my turn, that's all.'

One more knot attaching Arthur, one more attaching Billie. He pulled them both loose, and then another one, the last one attaching the bomb to the girder. The ropes slid free, and he tipped himself back. The ropes attaching him to the bomb still criss-crossed his body, and the weight of the bomb pulled him away from his friends' hands. Their fingers clutched at him, still trying to undo the knots around him.

But Harry carried on tipping backwards, and plummeted off the bridge.

Chapter Twenty

Harry fell towards the water.

His clothes whipped with the speed of his descent. The bomb hung underneath him with its heavier weight, speeding his fall. His fingers worked furiously, picking at the ropes that still tied his wrists. He sucked in air as fast as he could, knowing that he would need every scrap, every wisp. His ribs pushed out against the ropes as he tried to pull in another breath, but his lungs were still only half-full.

He plunged into the water, and that was the only air he had.

Down he went, dragged by the bomb. His clothes were still moving, but more slowly. They waved in the gloom, a fine mesh of bubbles rising from them. The river grew colder and darker the further he sank, and already his lungs were aching, desperate to breathe.

He concentrated on his fingers. They were red and

bleeding, the nails snapped, but at least the pain in them was fading as the river's cold deadened them. He forced them into the knots, which he found were a little looser, the water softening them. But Artie was right—Lord Jaspar had made these the most complicated knots of all. The ones around his wrists came slowly loose, and his hands dived to the one by his hip, working it free, and then scrabbled at one by his chest. It was tougher, and another nail split, blood seeping from the wound, warming his skin. He flinched, but kept pushing the finger in, and at last a loop formed, and he tugged it out. While one hand finished that job, another pulled free a small knot by his shoulder, and then grabbed another, the one looped around the top of his leg, and he was starting to work on it when he and the bomb thudded into the river bed.

Silt swirled up around him. The water darkened, and all he could see was mud and snaking riverweed. Harry scrabbled about in the silt, snatching at rocks and strands of weed. He saw a faint brightness far above him, the surface of the water. Was the bridge safe? It seemed so, with the bomb all the way down here.

But I'm down here, too.

He doubled over the knot. The action cramped his lungs, and he couldn't stop a silvery bubble escaping from his mouth. He probed the knot, checking its shape. His fingers grew colder, and his body weakened as the oxygen faded from it. His heart throbbed like a watery fist pounding in his chest, over and over again.

A loop came free, but only a little. Harry tugged harder, but his fingers were like ice, so he doubled up even more, and grabbed the knot in his teeth. Opening his lips allowed water to seep through, and it trickled down his throat as the remaining air turned stale in his lungs. His teeth bit harder, and he jerked his head from side to side, pulling the loop, his mouth filling with tastes of rope and mud.

The knot was gone. The loop had come free, and the rope drifted into the swirling silt, another tendril of riverweed. The other ropes fell away. Harry scrabbled his arms in the water and swam up, one of his boots brushing against the bomb, left in the silt. He tried to swim to the surface but his clothes hung heavily around him, slowing him down, furling and unfurling in the water, heavy and dark. Harry fought and kicked, but his clothes hardly moved at all now. The surface of the water shone above him, undulating gently with the river's ripples. His arms lifted and he saw ribbons of blood trail from his outstretched fingers. His legs kicked, and the effort forced the remains of air from his lungs.

His strength was gone. He waited for the weight of his clothes to drag him back down.

His hands broke through the surface. He felt cool, fluttering wind against his fingers, and then the palms of his hands. His arms followed, his head broke through too, and he sucked in air, its freshness stabbing into him. He howled, gasped, and looked up, shaking water from his eyes. *The bomb's about to go off—* he could tell that from the position of the train.

It was nearly halfway across the bridge. Its engine thundered, its wheels clattered. Seconds remained until it would arrive at the point where the bomb, Harry, and his friends had been tied. *How long was I under the water—a minute?* His body still weak, his heart still throbbing, he started to swim, trying to get as far away as he could from the bomb that was about to detonate directly below him.

'Get to the brick tower! It'll shield you!'

Billie and Arthur, high above him, clambered through the girders. They were nearly at one of the huge brick towers that supported the bridge, and that was where he was headed, too. His arms windmilled through the water, his legs kicked and, with a final push, he touched the solid brickwork and clambered up onto it. His bleeding fingers dug between the bricks and he pulled himself a little further up. Harry clung there, angling his head up at the train.

The engine had passed the spot. The first few

carriages had rattled past it too and, for an instant, Harry wondered if Lord Jaspar had miscalculated. But then he saw the lettering of a particular carriage, further down the train.

Dining Carriage. He almost smiled at the precision of it, as that particular carriage crossed the spot.

A thundering roar. It was as if a huge creature had been released upwards from the river, a vast watery mass with thrashing limbs, almost as high as the bridge above. The brick support shook, and Harry wondered if it might give way, toppling down brick by brick. But it held firm, and he watched the watery creature sink back down, its limbs flailing, its roar fading, its body dissolving into mist. It was gone, leaving the surface of the river boiling above it. Harry heard the train screech to a halt, but it had nearly reached the other side of the bridge, every last carriage of it. The squeal of the brakes faded and he heard different sounds: doors slamming open, windows rattling down. Faces peered out of the carriages, trying to see what had happened down in the river, and in amongst the criss-crossing iron girders of the Victoria Railway Bridge.

Chapter Twenty-one

Harry walked along a corridor of the St Pancras Hotel, past paintings of landscapes and London scenes, his boots sinking noiselessly into the rug. Ahead of him a pair of polished doors waited, with murmuring voices beyond it; beside him, Billie and Arthur hurried along. And behind the three of them, bustling along in a crowd of fluttering papers, clutching smelling-salt bottles, that pink monocle, and differently designed handkerchiefs, were the remaining members of the Benevolent Orphans.

'The sheer danger we were in!' gasped Professor Winterskill.

'To think, I had only just ordered a cup of tea from the dining-carriage trolley!' agreed Lady Brewster. 'A peaceful moment, but in reality we were entering the most deadly of snares!'

'A snare cunningly set over years—a whole decade,

it seems. These documents from Jaspar's office confirm it.' Sir Julian Elkins-Ford fumbled through papers as he marched along. 'A traitor lingering at our heart. All those meetings, all those conferences, all those discussions and yet we never detected him!'

'But our young friends did, in a trice,' said straggle-haired Professor Winterskill. His hands trembled slightly but he swallowed a pill and pushed open the doors for Harry and his friends. Harry heard ripples of applause as he stepped through into the hotel conference room. There they were again, the journalists lined up on the velvet-cushioned chairs, eagerly waiting for news. The Benevolent Orphans hurried up to the long table on the stage, Harry and his friends following.

'We didn't exactly solve it in a *trice*, Professor Winterskill,' Arthur said. 'It took us quite a few goes, actually.'

'We were wrong a lot more than we were right,' added Harry. 'Remember when we came to see you at breakfast, saying Magwell was behind it?'

'Better than being wrong for nearly a decade! Better than devoting years to a noble purpose, and not realizing a monster was exploiting it for his own gain!' Sir Julian dabbed his forehead with his Chinese dragon handkerchief, and then waved the file of papers again. 'That devil Jaspar—our leader, and yet he thought only of destroying our cause—and in the end, us as well!'

'But who will sit in Lord Jaspar's place now? One of us must be our new leader, but who?' Lady Brewster surveyed the seats along the table. The other Benevolent Orphans joined her, glancing between the different seats too, and in particular the one at the centre, the commanding spot.

'Why don't you just not have a leader?' Billie shrugged. 'That's how me, Harry, and Arthur run our little outfit.'

'It's true,' Arthur agreed. 'You all want the same thing. Why don't you run your slightly bigger outfit together? Take turns doing different things.'

The Benevolent Orphans stared, seeming genuinely surprised by this thought. But Harry barely glanced at them, looking at Billie instead, who had quietly taken one of his hands as she spoke. Arthur had taken the other one, and for a moment Harry just stood there, feeling the warmth of his friends' touch. *Our little outfit.* He remembered those hands, just a few hours ago, moving over him, desperately trying to release the knots securing him, even as his own hands tried to release the ones securing Billie and Arthur.

'Indeed, no leader! We shall henceforth operate

as a collective!' Lady Brewster declared firmly, sitting herself at the far end of the table. 'Let us incorporate it into our articles of association forthwith.'

'Yes, and let us conduct this press conference in a democratic way, too,' said Professor Winterskill, lowering himself into another chair. 'We shall take turns to answer questions. Never again shall we allow our organization to be taken over by a fiend like Jaspar—'

'But what has become of Lord Jaspar? Tell us!' a journalist yelled.

The Benevolent Orphans looked round at the assembled crowd and hesitated as they took in the gripped notebooks and clutched pens. Sir Julian invited Harry, Billie, and Arthur to join them and then nodded at Lady Brewster, indicating that she should answer the question. But she only nodded in turn to Professor Winterskill, who gestured back at Sir Julian again—and it was he who eventually leant forward and announced the vital fact.

'Fled to South America,' Sir Julian said. 'Not Argentina, though. When he heard his plan had failed, he raced for the nearest port and leapt aboard the first ship heading in that general direction—Uruguay.'

'And his plan will be different in another respect,' said Professor Winterskill, scrutinizing the papers from Jaspar's office. His pink monocle seemed to be causing him difficulty, and he snatched it from his eye and read on, unassisted. 'Simply, he will have no money whatsoever. Thanks to the fact that the critical clause transferring all our money to him on our deaths will never be activated, due to our not actually dying. No thanks to him!'

'And we have telegrammed our various contacts in the banking world, so that the money he already has—a considerable amount, due to our misguided trust in him—will be instantly recovered,' said Lady Brewster. 'He will be penniless when he disembarks in South America.'

'He will be that destitute orphan he was, all that time ago.' Sir Julian's handkerchiefs protruded from his various pockets, but he wasn't dabbing at his face with any of them. 'Once again, he will have to hatch some awful gruel-stealing plan, but he'll find it more difficult this time, thanks to Lady Brewster.'

'Yes, I have used my extensive publishing contacts to spread news of this awful villain's deeds,' Lady Brewster declared. 'Writers worldwide will discuss him! He will be notorious, I guarantee it. Gentlemen of the press, we also look to you to provide publicity. Expose the scoundrel! Hunt him down!'

'And not only him!' Professor Winterskill, not content with removing the monocle from his eye, tore it from the string that attached it to his jacket, and tossed it away. Then he pointed at the doors at the other end of the room. 'There are other murky fellows in this business, let us not forget.'

Inspector Newton had burst through the doors, a small group of policemen following behind. Harry's hands gripped the edge of the table, and he saw Arthur and Billie flinch as they remembered being locked in the Black Maria. But he noticed, as the burly inspector strode up the aisle, that he too seemed a little nervous, glancing at the journalists' poised pens. He arrived at the table, planted two fists on it, and leant towards Sir Julian.

'My congratulations on discovering the truth of this business,' Newton muttered, his voice a growled whisper. 'But, regarding how we present what has occurred, particularly to the gentlemen of the press, it must be managed carefully—'

'Oh it shall be, very carefully!' Sir Julian exclaimed into Newton's face, making the policeman rock back on his heels. 'Very carefully, but very loudly too!'

'There's no need to whisper, Inspector,' Winterskill glared with a new, steady focus. 'Proclamation, that is the order of the day. These affairs must be heard at volume! The very greatest volume, I should say!'

'The business of Ernest Magwell, the fact that he

was the origin of the appalling weapons used by Lord Jaspar on his murderous spree—is that what you wish to refer to in such hushed tones?' Lady Brewster glared too. 'Let me assure you we wish to use the publicity surrounding these events to further poor Dame Flora's work regarding Magwell and his shady dealings.'

'Lord Jaspar may have murdered her, but Magwell was her enemy as well. As he is the enemy of all right-thinking folk,' said Professor Winterskill. 'We have seen the destruction wreaked in London by his appalling bomb—imagine the havoc his weapons cause when delivered into the hands of someone like the king of Ravelstan, to pursue his cruel war. Despite a worldwide ban!'

'We'll take Magwell on, in Dame Flora's name! We shall expose his illegal, war-continuing ways!' Lady Brewster deliberately eyed the journalists, who were scribbling away. 'No matter how powerful his connections may be—do you not agree, Inspector Newton?'

'Powerful connections? I have no idea what you're implying,' said the policeman, backing away.

'I find that hard to believe. Perhaps we should speak at even greater volume, for clarity's sake?' Professor Winterskill scoffed. 'These theatre children understand perfectly well—do you not, Billie?'

'It's true. Magwell has friends in powerful places,

and that includes the police force.' Billie pointed at Newton. 'We tried to find out what was going on and you stopped us at every turn! You even arrested us!'

'I saw you at Magwell's factory, Inspector.' Harry made sure his words were clear, and he saw the journalists writing them down. 'You'd brought his bullet casings from the scene of Dame Flora's murder and you were discussing the case. Telling him he was safe, maybe? That the investigation would never come near him?'

'B-but I was right not to investigate him—there *was* no involvement by Magwell,' Newton stuttered at the Benevolent Orphans. 'It was your Lord Jaspar who—'

'Magwell wasn't involved in the murder but he's involved in plenty else,' Sir Julian cut him off. 'Illegal arms-dealing—what does it say of your police force that you seek to protect a powerful man like that? If only you had investigated as fearlessly as these children— as fearlessly as we Benevolent Orphans now intend to do! We shall probe every corner of Magwell's business! What other bans has he illegally defied? What other wars has he deliberately prolonged? We shall discover, and we shall prosecute him and his powerful friends with the full force of the law! Too many innocent people have suffered because of his wicked doings, and we shall come to their aid, as our society always does!

The rescue of others is a triumph for all—is there not some similar motto in your policeman's code?'

Possibly, thought Harry. But if there was, Newton had forgotten it, because his mouth hung silently open, his mutton-chop beard dangling. Even if there was a police motto, it clearly wasn't as stirring as the Benevolent Orphans' one, which was being noted down and repeated by the journalists, at the same time as they lifted their hands and asked more questions of the charitable donors and Inspector Newton. *But they'll have to hurry to get much out of him*, thought Harry, as Newton spun round and swept back out of the room.

Ahead, the doors were open. Harry saw a familiar shape out in the lobby, silhouetted against the light from the street outside. Tall, powerful, his legs apart, a dark cape with red lining hanging from his shoulders, his arms crossed commandingly. But as the furore from the journalists grew, and as Newton hurried out towards him, there was something entirely uncommanding about the way that figure swung away, the light catching the scars on his face. He half-turned back, but walked on again. Newton hurried after him and extended an arm, but Magwell threw it off with some force. He strode onwards across the lobby, and stormed into the spinning wood and glass of the hotel's revolving doors.

'Just a loose end, really,' Billie said to Harry and Arthur. 'He wasn't anything to do with it, like Sir Julian said.'

'That's true. At the same time, I'm not sure Magwell's going to find it so easy running an arms business from now on—not in London, anyway,' said Arthur, nodding at the journalists. The Benevolent Orphans are after him—and a whole press campaign's underway.'

'A loose end all right,' said Harry. 'But still worth tying up.'

'We did pretty well getting that done too, along with everything else. In fact, we did pretty well generally,' said Arthur, and leant close to Harry. 'Especially you.'

Billie leant close too and Harry stopped paying attention to the press conference. All he could see was his friends' faces, so close together they were almost touching; all he could hear were their voices, whispering in that little space.

'Did you know you'd be able to undo the knots in time, Harry?' Billie was asking. 'When you decided— when you threw yourself and the bomb off the bridge?'

'I knew I could save you and the Benevolent Orphans,' Harry said.

'That's not really an answer to her question.' Arthur frowned.

'It sort of is,' said Harry. 'Everyone thinks that the hardest you'll fight is if you're trying to save your own life. But it's not true, I think. Not for me, anyway. Not for any of us three. Billie, when you grabbed the lid of the soup tureen and bounced the grenade into the soup—could you really have pulled that off unless you weren't just saving yourself, but me, Artie, and all the other folk in the theatre?'

'I suppose you're right,' said Billie, quietly.

'And Artie, when you were undoing the knots on the bridge, the ones you undid fastest weren't the ones tying you, they were the ones round me,' Harry said. 'I saw that for sure.'

'Maybe that's true.' Arthur looked at his hands. 'I nearly tore my fingers apart.'

'It goes for the whole investigation—the reason we were brave enough to carry on with it, however dangerous it got, was because we knew how important it was.' The words raced out even faster. 'We knew the Benevolent Orphans were depending on it, and all the people they help—the hospitals, the schools, the libraries, the people who suffer in wars, everyone. It mattered to us more than anything, and it mattered to me, when I was up on that bridge. All those lives at stake, and your lives, too—that was what I was thinking of.' That knot again, deep in his throat. 'And *that's* how I knew I'd be able to pull free of those ropes in time.'

They understood. Harry could see that from their eyes, and from the way that, apart from the odd mutter, they had hardly spoken a word. Anyone else would have stopped him, asked questions, tried to disagree, but not Arthur and Billie; why would they, when they had been up on that bridge too? For a little longer, the three of them sat there, thinking it all through, remembering those incredible moments as the bomb ticked and the train thundered closer . . .

And then Harry wasn't thinking of the past at all. He was thinking of the future, as he heard a familiar sound, somewhere nearby in the hotel.

The ringing of a telephone. It rang a few more times, and then cut out. Shortly afterwards, a hotel servant appeared in the doorway and hurried forward. Harry heard him whisper in Sir Julian's ear.

'A telephone call for your young friends, Sir Julian.'

Chapter Twenty-two

Harry and his friends followed the servant into the next room. Harry took the receiver, Arthur and Billie gathered around him, and they waited for the servant to close the door behind him.

'Hello?' said Harry, into the telephone.

'The usual precautions,' said the familiar voice. 'Although this time, I believe there's a fair chance of locating me—'

'Across the street, five storeys up,' said Billie, staring out through a window at a building nearby. Framed in one of its windows was a pale-suited figure, just near enough for it to be seen that he was holding a telephone. *Mr James of the Order of the White Crow.* Harry picked out that neatly trimmed white beard, those grey eyes. The mysterious gentleman whom he had first seen from a Manhattan tightrope, the mysterious gentleman who was behind it all.

'Well spotted, Billie,' the voice crackled on. 'But few are as observant as you and so I hope our conversation will remain private. Mind you, the three of you have drawn considerable attention to yourselves—the hope was that you would remain invisible, unknown.'

'That's hard to do if you're detonating a powerful bomb in the middle of London, Mr James,' Arthur said.

'An acute observation, Arthur,' the voice replied. 'It's difficult to see how you could have been secretive about *many* of the events that have occurred during this investigation—a grenade in a soup tureen, a narrowly avoided assassination attempt in a roof garden, an escape from a burning Black Maria, to name but a few. To think that these remarkable feats have all been achieved by mere children—extraordinary.'

'Not particularly, Mr James,' Billie said. 'Not when it's children like us.'

Those twitching sensations, those flickers. They were back again, travelling all over Harry's skin. *Strange*—all he was doing was holding a telephone receiver in a London hotel. But he looked at his friends, and he could see that they were feeling something too, Arthur twirling his fountain pen in his hand, Billie flexing her fingers as she stared out the window.

'That's an acute observation as well, Billie.' The

figure adjusted its position. 'Although it takes us to another question—the three of you are far from being ordinary, but why is it that you have turned out so? I touched on this a couple of days ago, but my curiosity continues. Perhaps it really is what the Benevolent Orphans say: that those who overcome a difficult start in life often end up wanting to help others? That would make sense. Arthur, the boy who grew up in dusty library corridors; Billie, the girl who at too young an age travelled the length of America alone; and then there's Harry, a boy separated from his family for reasons no one yet understands, forced to fend for himself on the streets of New York, surviving by his wits and a lucky ability to pick up the odd magic trick . . . '

The static swarmed. Harry held the receiver closer and tried to decipher the words, just as he had tried to do on the train in Southampton, and during several conversations with Mr James before that. But the static was too thick and Harry suspected that, even if the voice had been perfectly clear, Mr James might have been hard to understand anyway, as he tried to explain what had happened over the last few days.

And it's pretty much been explained already, Harry thought. By those words spoken just a few moments ago, between him and his friends.

'All in good time.' Mr James's voice burst through

again. 'For now, we must concentrate on what is in front of you. What that actually *is*, I don't know—I have yet to receive instructions from the Order of the White Crow. But that won't take long. May I suggest that you return to the theatre, and continue performing your remarkable tricks? That upside-down rope one, perhaps? Or maybe something new. Performing your magic act seems a useful cover while you prepare for your next investigation . . . '

Harry held the earpiece away, and turned to his friends. The static was back, the words were faint, but a few had been plain enough, and those were the only ones they needed. *Your next investigation . . .* Arthur was twiddling his fountain pen faster, and Billie was flexing her fingers faster. He raised an eyebrow at them, but they were already nodding and smiling. Harry looked back at that pale-suited figure in the window, and spoke into the receiver.

'We'll head back to the theatre and get ready, Mr James,' he said. 'For our next trick.'

Enjoyed *The Silent Assassin*?
Read on for a taste of where
Harry's adventures all
began, in

Chapter One

The train was coming. Harry could see the puffs of
blackened steam rising over a row of broken-down
houses. He could hear the clatter of the engine. Down
by his feet vibrations were wobbling along the iron rails
and the ragged hems of his trousers were wobbling

too. *Won't be long now.* He stood there a little longer, his boot polish-stained fingers twitching, his eyes narrowing in the direction of the thundering roar.

He tugged a sturdy-looking padlock out of his jacket pocket and carried on chaining himself to the spot in the middle of the track.

'You've really lost it this time, Harry!'

'Harry! Are you absolutely sure about this?'

A boy and a girl stood just a few paces away. Billie, the girl, wore a ragged, glue-spattered factory smock, and she was casually leaning against a concrete stump, her head on one side, an eyebrow raised. *Typical, not even the tiniest bit impressed,* thought Harry with a smile, glancing across at the boy, who was a far more satisfying sight. Arthur was completely beside himself with excitement, hopping from foot to foot, his neatly tailored tweed suit flapping, his hands racing through a copy of the *New York City Train Timetable*.

'Do you really think this is a good idea, Harry? My calculations have turned out right, you see.' Stitches popped in the tweed suit and the younger boy's tie swirled as he flung an arm towards the puffs of smoke. 'That's the 15:24 from Grand Central. Which by my estimate is due to hit this exact spot . . .' He tugged a fob-watch from his waistcoat, dangled it in front of his face, and stared at it with eyes the size of half-dollar coins. 'In exactly two minutes, twenty-seven seconds' time!'

'So we have to hurry, Artie!' Harry looped a chain around his left leg, pulled it up round his head, and adjusted it so that it was at a jaunty angle. He heard his voice echo around, still full of the accent of his faraway Hungarian home, so different from his friend's English tones. 'Good job on the calculations but I'm not even properly manacled yet! Another chain, Billie?'

'One of the real heavy ones? Or perhaps something a little lighter, *sir*?' Another grin, and Billie pushed off the concrete stump, reached into the sack at her feet, and yanked out a clinking length of iron. 'I managed to find you a nice selection, heavy ones, light ones, that sort of thing . . .' Her voice bounced along with drawls and twangs as she swung the chain about a bit. 'Any other deadly situations you'd like me and Artie to rustle up for you? Dangle you by a rope off Brooklyn Bridge? Or smuggle you into the lion's cage at the City Zoo, maybe? We're getting pretty good now, I'm sure we could fix it . . .'

'You'd do a great job, both of you, but can we talk about it later?' Harry wrapped the chain around his middle, making sure that it too was at a jaunty angle. 'Let's just concentrate on the Great Train—'

'The Great Train Escape, I know.' Billie's left

eyebrow lifted a little higher. 'Hey Artie, seeing as we're busy with trains today, did I ever tell you about my own brush with one? The Louisiana Express Hay Wagon Ride, that's what I call it, and it was pretty rough—'

'There's no time, Billie!' Harry slid the padlock through the links.

'Sure there's time! So, I was desperate for a ride and so I hung out on a bridge near a goods station, waiting. When the train rattled underneath with a load of wagons of hay, I just jumped down! Nearly broke a leg!' Billie reached behind her back, pulled round the little ukulele she kept strapped there, and started strumming a tune. 'But that's what it's like on the road, you've got to grab any chance you can. So there I was, riding all the way to Arkansas, strumming my uke and—'

'Billie! Not now! Everyone's waiting. Look!'

Harry snapped the padlock shut and managed to jerk his head towards the rabble of about fifteen people lined up along the top of the bank on the far side of the tracks, framed against the blue September sky. Passers-by, shopkeepers, and even a couple of washerwomen— Billie and Arthur had spent nearly an hour drumming them up by racing around the surrounding streets, and every one of them seemed gripped by what was going on, their gazes fixed in his direction. *They'll stare even harder now,* Harry thought, as he plucked the key from the padlock and sent it flying through the air. It vanished into a patch of thorny bushes some distance away.

'You've really done it now.' Billie's ukulele playing stopped. Even she was looking impressed, staring after the key.

'Exactly!' Harry jerked his head towards the crowd. 'That's what everyone's thinking!'

'Yes, but you really *have* done it!' Arthur was a highspeed hopping, page-flicking, watch-waggling blur. 'We'll never be able to find it in all those thorns!'

'It's all part of the act.' Harry breathed deeply, and stared at the padlock as hard as he could. 'Look, I shouldn't really be talking—I'm meant to be pretending to have magical powers.'

He carried on doing just that. The clattering roar was louder now, the rails were vibrating faster, his ragged trouser-hems were flapping faster too, but he didn't bother about any of those things. Instead, he carried on staring at the chains with that deliberately mysterious gaze. He even tugged the padlock up to his mouth and muttered to it. *See a boy free himself through the speaking of ancient charms,* that was what Billie and Arthur had told the crowd—and, from the excited gasps he could hear drifting from the bank, it sounded like his audience was well on the way to believing it too. He kept muttering to the padlock, deliberately using phrases of Hungarian, knowing that the unfamiliar words would sound particularly mysterious to the listening crowd. He muttered even louder, and made his eyes roll about, pretending to lose himself completely in a magical trance, even as he detected faint odours of oil and soot, curling up his nose . . .

'The train! The train!'

Harry's eyes stopped rolling. They flicked towards the crowd. Every one of those fifteen heads had swiveled to the left because the train had shot out from behind the houses and was curving steadily around the track. Arms pointed, faces turned white. The engine, a hurtling bulk of iron, was still several hundred yards away, but steam shrieked from it as it clanged along the rails, and it was gathering speed. Harry watched it. The odours of oil and soot weren't just curling up his nose now, they were snaking down into his mouth, flavouring the spit trickling down his throat. *Time to get a move on.* But he couldn't resist squeezing in just a bit more bug-eyed magical staring at the chains.

'Harry! You've left it too late!'

A yell from Arthur as he raced for the thorny bushes. Billie was pulling off a well-rehearsed swoon, tottering about with the back of a hand against her forehead. *Nicely done,* thought Harry, as he watched Billie collapse onto the gravel; meanwhile Artie arrived at the bush and started rooting about as if all was lost. *All part of the act.* Still, they had been right earlier— there *wasn't* any way they could find the key and run back to set him free before the train hit. The thought made the chains holding him in place feel particularly heavy. Under his threadbare shirt, he felt a drop of sweat glide down between his shoulder blades. *Yes, time to get a move on* . . .

'Stop the train!'

'Somebody DO something!'

Screams from the crowd. One of the washerwomen had dropped her basket, the clothes inside tumbling down the bank, but no one seemed to have noticed. *Utterly gripped.* More drops of sweat were gathering now, on his forehead, his neck, under his arms, and Harry could feel strange little twitches quivering through his body. *Good*—every twitch, every drop of sweat would help him concentrate on the trick that lay ahead.

He lifted the padlock to his mouth again and muttered a bit more of that spell. He surrounded the padlock with his hands so no one would see the tiny bulge in his upper lip as his tongue curled up inside. Harry closed his eyes and felt his tongue deftly fetch down the little bent nail that was lodged there and nudge it around until it was gripped between his teeth. The bent end poked out of the corner of his mouth and he shot it into the padlock's keyhole.

Concentrate.

Harry tilted his head. He had carefully bent the nail so it fitted the padlock perfectly. He had practised endless times, first with his hands, then with his mouth. But he still felt his jaw shudder slightly as it shifted so that the nail angled upwards. His brain throbbed with the clatter of iron wheels, the shriek of steam. *Concentrate, concentrate.* He stared straight at the train, just a hundred yards away now, as he carried on picking the lock. And then the nail slipped.

Unexpectedly, the padlock had jerked to the left, tugging the nail from his teeth. For a couple of seconds, the little length of metal balanced precariously on his lower lip. He felt his whole body turn cold as he tried, with his tongue, to fetch it back. His vision blurred and he realized that his eyes had crossed, struggling to hold the nail in view as it balanced such a short distance away. His tongue strained, the twitches raced through every part of him.

Concentrate.

The nail was back between his teeth. He shot it back into the lock again, his jaw re-angling. He checked the train, which had jammed on its brakes but was hurtling forward anyway, an iron blur, just forty yards away. *Thirty, twenty.* The brakes screeched but all he could hear was, from deep inside the padlock, the stretching of tiny springs, the grind of tiny levers.

Then, echoing out of the keyhole, a click.

The clasp sprang open. The chains, heavy and cold, slithered away from him. One of them snagged on his left elbow but he shook it off, shaking off the other chains too, sending them flying away from the track. He looked up and saw the train's vast front, racing up to him. His legs, he had to admit, were a little less steady than usual, but he managed to spring into the air, just in time, and thudded onto the gravel next to the tracks.

He tucked the nail back inside his lip. Briefly, he remembered that troubling moment when it had dangled so precariously, and took in a shaky breath. But then he jumped up, brushing the dust from his clothes. He stumbled away from the track, his ragged clothes billowing in the thundering breeze of the train's wagons as they clattered past, picking up speed again. Ahead of him was the crowd. Everyone was clapping, cheering, waving hats in the air, throwing coins in his direction; Harry stopped walking and stood there for some time, watching the coins land. The train was gone now, but he still stood there. His vision blurred, and for a while he stopped thinking of anything apart from his still-pounding heart, his still-trembling body. Then he felt something jab him in his side.

'Harry? We are *here*, you know?'

It was Billie. She was standing next to him, laughing, and it was her elbow that was doing the jabbing, quite hard. Harry blinked, and then looked round at Arthur, who was on his other side, a smile on his face too.

'Sorry.' Harry blinked again, and felt his face grow warm. 'Sometimes takes me a bit of time to come round . . .'

'Don't worry, we're used to it.' Billie rolled her eyes.

'Thanks.' Harry held out his hands. 'So anyway— let's give them what they want, shall we?'

He waited for his friends to grab his hands. Then, together with them, he performed the move that he had practised more than any other.

A slow, elegant bow.

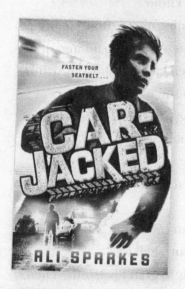

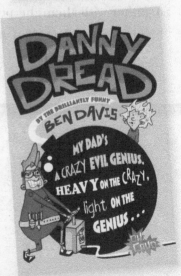